FAR-AWAY STORIES

Ladies in Lavender and other stories

BY

WILLIAM J. LOCKE

TO THE READER

DEAR SIR OR MADAM:—

Good wine needs no bush, but a collection of mixed vintages does. And this book is just such a collection. Some of the stories I do not want to remain buried forever in the museum files of dead magazine-numbers—an author's not unpardonable vanity; others I have resuscitated from the same vaults in the hope that they still may please you.

The title of a volume of short stories is always a difficult matter. It ought to indicate frankly the nature of the book so that the unwary purchaser shall have no grievance (except on the score of merit, which is a different affair altogether) against either author or publisher. In my title I have tried to solve the problem. But why "Far-away?" Well, the stories cover a long stretch of years, and all, save one, were written in calm days far-away from the present convulsion of the world.

Anyhow, no one will buy the book under the impression that it is a novel, and, finding that it isn't, revile me as a cheat. And so I have the pleasure of offering it for your perusal with a clear conscience.

You, Dear Sir or Madam, have given me, this many a year, an indulgence beyond my deserts. Till now, I have had no opportunity of thanking you. I do now with a grateful heart, and to you, I dedicate the two stories that I love the best, hoping that they may excuse those for which you may not so much care and that they may win continuance of that which is to me, both as a writer and as a human being, my most cherished possession, namely, your favorable regard for

Your most humble and obedient Servant to command,

W. J. LOCKE June 1919

THE SONG OF LIFE

Non cuivis homini contingit adire Corinthum. It is not everybody's good fortune to go to Corinth. It is also not everybody's good fortune to go to Peckham—still less to live there. But if you were one of the favored few, and were wont to haunt the Peckham Road and High Street, the bent figure of Angelo Fardetti would have been as familiar to you as the vast frontage of the great Emporium which, in the drapery world, makes Peckham illustrious among London suburbs. You would have seen him humbly threading his way through the female swarms that clustered at the plate-glass windows—the mere drones of the hive were fooling their frivolous lives away over ledgers in the City—the inquiry of a lost dog in his patient eyes, and an unconscious challenge to Philistia in the wiry bush of white hair that protruded beneath his perky soft felt hat. If he had been short, he might have passed unregarded; but he was very tall—in his heyday, he had been six foot two—and very thin. You smile as you recall to mind the black frock-coat, somewhat white at the seams, which, tightly buttoned, had the fit of a garment of corrugated iron. Although he was so tall one never noticed the inconsiderable stretch of trouser below the long skirt. He always appeared to be wearing a truncated cassock. You were inclined to laugh at this queer exotic of the Peckham Road until you looked more keenly at the man himself. Then you saw an old, old face, very swarthy, very lined, very beautiful still in its regularity of feature, maintaining in a little white mustache with waxed ends a pathetic braggadocio of youth; a face in which the sorrows of the world seemed to have their dwelling, but sorrows that on their way thither had passed through the crucible of a simple soul.

Twice a day it was his habit to walk there; shops and faces a meaningless confusion to his eyes, but his ears alert to the many harmonies of the orchestra of the great thoroughfare. For Angelo Fardetti was a musician. Such had he been born; such had he lived. Those aspects of life which could not be interpreted in terms of music were to him unintelligible. During his seventy years, empires had crumbled, mighty kingdoms had arisen, bloody wars had been fought, magic conquests been made by man over nature. But none of these convulsive facts had ever stirred Angelo Fardetti's imagination. Even his country he had well-nigh forgotten; it was so many years since he had left it, so much music had passed since then through his being. Yet he had never learned to speak English correctly; and, not having an adequate language (save music) in which to clothe his thoughts, he spoke very little. When addressed he smiled at you sweetly like a pleasant, inarticulate old child.

Though his figure was so familiar to the inhabitants of Peckham, few knew how and where he lived. As a matter of fact, he lived a few hundred yards away from the busy High Street, in Formosa Terrace, at the house of one Anton Kirilov, a musician. He had lodged with the Kirilovs for over twenty years—but not always in the roomy splendor of Formosa Terrace. Once Angelo was the first violin in an important orchestra, a man of mark, while Anton fiddled away in the obscurity of a fifth-rate music-hall. Then the famous violinist rented the drawing-room floor of the Kirilovs' little house in Clapham, while the Kirilovs, humble folk, got on as best they could. Now things had changed. Anton Kirilov was musical director of a London theatre, but Angelo, through age and rheumatism and other infirmities, could fiddle in public no more; and so it came to pass that Anton Kirilov and Olga, his wife, and Sonia, their daughter (to whom Angelo had stood godfather twenty years ago), rioted in spaciousness, while the old man lodged in tiny rooms at the top of the house, paying an infinitesimal rent and otherwise living on his scanty savings and such few shillings as he could earn by copying out parts and giving lessons to here and there a snubnosed little girl in a tradesman's back parlor. Often he might have gone without sufficient nourishment had not Mrs. Kirilov seen to it; and whenever an extra good dish, succulent and strong, appeared at her table, either Sonia or the servant carried a plateful upstairs with homely compliments.

"You are making of me a spoiled child, Olga," he would say sometimes, "and I ought not to eat of the food for which Anton works so hard."

And she would reply with a laugh:

"If we did not keep you alive, Signor Fardetti, how should we have our quarters on Sunday afternoons?"

You see, Mrs. Kirilov, like the good Anton, had lived all her life in music too—she was a pianist, and Sonia also was a musician—she played the 'cello in a ladies' orchestra. So they had famous Sunday quarters at Formosa Terrace, in which Fardetti was well content to play second fiddle to Anton's first.

You see, also, that but for these honest souls to whom a musician like Fardetti was a sort of blood-brother, the evening of the old man's days might have been one of tragic sadness. But even their affection and his glad pride in the brilliant success of his old pupil, Geoffrey Chase, could not mitigate the one great sorrow of his life. The violin, yes; he had played it well; he had not aimed at a great soloist's fame, for want of early training, and he had never dreamed such unrealizable dreams, but other dreams had he dreamed with passionate intensity. He had dreamed of being a great composer, and he had beaten his heart out against the bars that shut him from the great mystery. A waltz or two, a few songs, a catchy march, had been published and performed, and had brought him unprized money and a little hateful repute; but the compositions into which he had poured his soul remained in dusty manuscript, despised and rejected of musical men.

For many years the artist's imperious craving to create and hope and will kept him serene. Then, in the prime of his days, a tremendous inspiration shook him. He had a divine message to proclaim to the world, a song of life itself, a revelation. It was life, indestructible, eternal. It was the seed that grew into the tree; the tree that flourished lustily, and then grew bare and stark and perished; the seed, again, of the tree that rose unconquerable into the laughing leaf of spring. It was the kiss of lovers that, when they were dead and gone, lived immortal on the lips of grandchildren. It was the endless roll of the seasons, the majestic, triumphant rhythm of existence. It was a cosmic chant, telling of things as only music could tell of them, and as no musician had ever told of them before.

He attempted the impossible, you will say. He did. That was the pity of it. He spent the last drop of his heart's blood over his sonata. He wrote it and rewrote it, wasting years, but never could he imprison within those remorseless ruled lines the elusive sounds that shook his being. An approximation to his dream reached the stage of a completed score. But he knew that it was thin and lifeless. The themes that were to be developed into magic harmonies tinkled into commonplace. The shell of this vast conception was there, but the shell alone. The thing could not live without the unseizable, and that he had not seized. Angelo Fardetti, broken down by toil and misery, fell very sick. Doctors recommended Brighton. Docile as a child, he went to Brighton, and they're a pretty lady who admired his playing at the Monday Popular Concerts at St. James's Hall, got hold of him and married him. When she ran away, a year later, with a dashing young stockbroker, he took the score of the sonata that was to be the whole interpretation of life from its half-forgotten hiding-place, played it through on the piano, burst into a passion of tears, in the uncontrollable Italian way, sold up his house, and went to lodge with Anton Kirilov. To no son or daughter of man did he ever show a note or play a bar of the sonata. And never again did he write a line of music. Bravely and humbly he faced life, though the tragedy of failure made him prematurely old. And all through the years the sublime message reverberated in his soul and haunted his dreams; and his was the bitter sorrow of knowing that never should that message be delivered for the comforting of the world.

The loss of his position as first violin forced him, at sixty, to take more obscure engagements. That was when he followed the Kirilovs to Peckham. And then he met the joy of his old age—his one pupil of genius, Geoffrey Chase, an untrained lad of fourteen, the son of a well-to-do seed merchant in the High Street.

"His father thinks it a waste of time," said Mrs. Chase, a gentle, mild-eyed woman, when she brought the boy to him, "but Geoffrey is so set on it—and so I've persuaded his father to let him have lessons."

"Do you, too, love music?" he asked.

Her eyes grew moist, and she nodded.

"Poor lady! He should not let you starve. Never mind," he said, patting her shoulder. "Take comfort. I will teach your boy to play for you."

And he did. He taught him for three years. He taught him passionately all he knew, for Geoffrey, with music in his blood, had the great gift of the composer. He poured upon the boy all the love of his lonely old heart and dreamed glorious dreams of his future. The Kirilovs, too, regarded Geoffrey as a prodigy, and welcomed him into their circle, and made much of him. And little Sonia fell in love with him, and he, in his boyish way, fell in love with the dark-haired maiden who played on a 'cello so much bigger than herself. At last, the time came when Angelo said:

"My son, I can teach you no more. You must go to Milan."

"My father will never consent," said Geoffrey.

"We will try to arrange that," said Angelo.

So, in their simple ways, Angelo and Mrs. Chase intrigued together until they prevailed upon Mr. Chase to attend one of the Kirilovs' Sunday concerts. He came in church-going clothes, and sat with irreconcilable stiffness on a straight-backed chair. His wife sat close by, much agitated. The others played a concerto arranged as a quintette; Geoffrey first violin, Angelo second, Sonia 'cello, Anton bass, and Mrs. Kirilov at the piano. It was a piece of exquisite tenderness and beauty.

"Very pretty," said Mr. Chase.

"It's beautiful," cried his wife, with tears in her eyes.

"I said so," remarked Mr. Chase.

"And what do you think of my pupil?" Angelo asked excitedly.

"I think he plays very nicely," Mr. Chase admitted.

"But, dear heavens!" cried Angelo. "It is not his playing! One could pick up fifty better violinists in the street. It is the concerto—the composition."

Mr. Chase rose slowly to his feet. "Do you mean to tell me that Geoffrey made up all that himself?"

"Of course. Didn't you know?"

"Will you play it again?"

Gladly they assented. When it was over he took Angelo out into the passage.

"I'm not one of those narrow-minded people who don't believe in art, Mr. Fardetti," said he. "And Geoff has already shown me that he can't sell seeds for toffee. But if he takes up music, will he be able to earn his living at it?"

"Beyond doubt," replied Angelo, with a wide gesture.

"But a good living? You'll forgive me being personal, Mr. Fardetti, but you yourself——"

"I," said the old man humbly, "am only a poor fiddler—but your son is a great musical genius."

"I'll think over it," said Mr. Chase.

Mr. Chase thought over it, and Geoffrey went to Milan, and Angelo Fardetti was once more left desolate. On the day of the lad's departure he and Sonia wept a little in each other's arms, and late that night he once more unearthed the completed score of his sonata and scanned it through in vain hope of comfort. But as the months passed comfort came. His beloved swan was not a goose, but a wonder among swans. He was a wonder at the Milan Conservatoire and won prize after prize and medal after medal, and every time he came home he bore his blushing honors thicker upon him. And he remained the same frank, simple youth, always filled with gratitude and reverence for his old master, and though on familiar student terms with all conditions of cosmopolitan damsels, never faithless to the little Anglo-Russian maiden whom he had left at home.

In the course of time his studies were over, and he returned to England. A professorship at the Royal School of Music very soon rendered him financially independent. He began to create. Here and there a piece of his was played at concerts. He wrote incidental music for solemn productions at great London theatres. Critics discovered him, and wrote much about him in the newspapers. Mr. Chase, the seed merchant, though professing to his wife a man-of-the-world's indifference to notoriety, used surreptitiously to cut out the notices and carry them about in his fat pocket-book, and whenever he had a new one he would lie in wait for the lean figure of Angelo Fardetti, and hale him into the shop and make him drink Geoffrey's health in sloe gin, which Angelo abhorred, but gulped down in honour of the prodigy.

One fine October morning Angelo Fardetti missed his walk. He sat instead by his window, and looked unseeingly at the prim row of houses on the opposite side of Formosa Terrace. He had not the heart to go out—and, indeed, he had not the money; for these walks, twice daily, along the High Street and the Peckham Road, took him to and from a queer little Italian restaurant which, with him apparently as its only client, had eked out for years a mysterious and precarious existence. He felt very old— he was seventy-two, very useless, very poor. He had lost his last pupil, a fat, unintelligent girl of thirteen, the daughter of a local chemist, and no one had sent him any copying work for a week. He had nothing to do. He could not even walk to his usual sparrow's meal. It is sad when you are so old that you cannot earn the right to live in a world which wants you no longer.

Looking at unseen bricks through a small window-pane was little consolation. Mechanically he rose and went to a grand piano, his one possession of price, which, with an old horsehair sofa, an oval table covered with a maroon cloth, and a chair or two, congested the tiny room, and, sitting down, began to play one of Stephen Heller's *Nuits Blanches*. You see, Angelo Fardetti was an old-fashioned musician. Suddenly a phrase arrested him. He stopped dead and remained staring out over the polished plane of the piano. For a few moments, he was lost in the chain of associated musical ideas. Then suddenly his swarthy, lined face lit up, and he twirled his little white mustache and began to improvise, striking great majestic chords. Presently he rose, and from a pile of loose music in a corner drew a sheet of ruled paper. He returned to the piano and began feverishly to pencil down his inspiration. His pulses throbbed. At last he had got the great andante movement of his sonata. For an hour he worked intensely; then came the inevitable check. Nothing more would come. He rose and walked about the room, his head swimming. After a quarter of an hour he played over what he had written, and then, with a groan of despair, fell forward, his arms on the keys, his bushy white head on his arms.

The door opened, and Sonia, comely and shapely, entered the room, carrying a tray with food and drink set out on a white cloth. Seeing him bowed over the piano, she put the tray on the table and advanced.

"Dear godfather," she said gently, her hand on his shoulder.

He raised his head and smiled.

"I did not hear you, my little Sonia."

"You have been composing?"

He sat upright, and tore the penciled sheets into fragments, which he dropped in a handful on the floor.

"Once, long ago, I had a dream. I lost it. To-day I thought that I had found it. But do you know what I did really find?"

"No, godfather," replied Sonia, stooping, with housewifely tidiness, to pick up the litter.

"That I am a poor old fool," said he.

Sonia threw the paper into the grate and again came up behind him.

"It is better to have lost a dream than never to have had one at all. What was your dream?"

"I thought I could write the Song of Life as I heard it—as I hear it still." He smote his forehead lightly. "But no! God has not considered me worthy to sing it. I bow my head to His—to His"—he sought for the word with thin fingers—"to His decree."

She said, with the indulgent wisdom of youth speaking to age:

"He has given you the power to love and to win love."

The old man swung round on the music-stool and put his arm around her waist and smiled into her young face.

"Geoffrey is a very fortunate fellow."

"Because he's a successful composer?"

He looked at her and shook his head, and Sonia, knowing what he meant, blushed very prettily. Then she laughed and broke away.

"Mother has had seventeen partridges sent her as presents this week, and she wants you to help her eat them, and father's offered a bargain in some good Beaujolais, and won't decide until you tell him what you think of it."

Deftly she set out the meal and drew a chair to the table. Angelo Fardetti rose.

"That I should love you all," said he simply, "is only human, but that you should so much love me is more than I can understand."

You see, he knew that watchful ears had missed his usual outgoing footsteps, and that watchful hearts had divined the reason. To refuse, to hesitate would be to reject love. So there was no more to be said. He sat down meekly, and Sonia ministered to his wants. As soon as she saw that he was making headway with the partridge and the burgundy, she too sat by the table.

"Godfather," she said, "I've had splendid news this morning."

"Geoffrey?"

"Of course. What other news could be splendid? His Symphony in E flat is going to be given at the Queen's Hall."

"That is indeed beautiful news," said the old man, laying down knife and fork, "but I did not know that he had written a Symphony in E flat."

"That was why he went and buried himself for months in Cornwall—to finish it," she explained.

"I knew nothing about it. Aie! aie!" he sighed. "It is to you, and no longer to me, that he tells things."

"You silly, jealous old dear!" she laughed. "He *had* to account for deserting me all the summer. But as to what it's all about, I'm as ignorant as you are. I've not heard a note of it. Sometimes Geoff is like that, you know. If he's dead certain sure of himself, he won't have any criticism or opinions while the work's in progress. It's only when he's doubtful that he brings one in. And the doubtful things are never anything like the certain ones. You must have noticed it."

"That is true," said Angelo Fardetti, taking up knife and fork again. "He was like that since he was a boy."

"It is going to be given on Saturday fortnight. He'll conduct himself. They've got a splendid programme to send him off. Lembrich's going to play, and Carli's going to sing—just for his sake. Isn't it gorgeous?"

"It is grand. But what does Geoffrey say about it? Come, come, after all he is not the sphinx." He drummed his fingers impatiently on the table.

"Would you really like to know?"

"I am waiting."

"He says it's going to knock 'em!" she laughed.

"Knock 'em?"

"Those were his words."

"But——"

She interpreted into purer English. Geoffrey was confident that his symphony would achieve a sensational success.

"In the meanwhile," said she, "if you don't finish your partridge you'll break mother's heart."

She poured out a glass of burgundy, which the old man drank; but he refused the food.

"No, no," he said, "I cannot eat more. I have a lump there—in my throat. I am too excited. I feel that he is marching to his great triumph. My little Geoffrey." He rose, knocking his chair over, and strode about the confined space. "*Sacramento*! But I am a wicked old man. I was sorrowful because I was so dull, so stupid that I could not write a sonata. I blamed the good God. *Mea maxima culpa*. And at once he sends me a partridge in a halo of love, and the news of my dear son's glory——"

Sonia stopped him, her plump hands on the front of his old corrugated frock-coat.

"And your glory, too, dear godfather. If it hadn't been for you, where would Geoffrey be? And who realises it more than Geoffrey? Would you like to see a bit of his letter? Only a little bit—for there's a lot of rubbish in it that I would be ashamed of anybody who thinks well of him to read—but just a little bit."

Her hand was at the broad belt joining blouse and skirt. Angelo, towering above her, smiled with an old man's tenderness at the laughing love in her dark eyes, and at the happiness in her young, comely face. Her features were generous, and her mouth frankly large, but her lips were fresh and her teeth white and even, and to the old fellow she looked all that man could dream of the virginal mother-to-be of great sons. She fished the letter from her belt, scanned and folded it carefully.

"There! Read."

And Angelo Fardetti read:

"I've learned my theory and technique, and God knows what —things that only they could teach me—from professors with world-famous names. But for real inspiration, for the fount of music itself, I come back all the time to our dear old *maestro*, Angelo Fardetti. I can't for the life of me define what it is, but he opened for me a secret chamber behind whose concealed door all these illustrious chaps have walked unsuspectingly. It seems silly to say it because, beyond a few odds and ends, the dear old man has composed nothing, but I am convinced that I owe the essentials of everything I do in music to his teaching and influence."

Angelo gave her back the folded letter without a word, and turned and stood again by the window, staring unseeingly at the prim, semi-detached villas opposite. Sonia, having re-hidden her treasure, stole up to him. Feeling her near, he stretched out a hand and laid it on her head.

"God is very wonderful," said he—"very mysterious. Oh, and so good!"

He fumbled, absently and foolishly, with her well-ordered hair, saying nothing more. After a while, she freed herself gently and led him back to his partridge.

A day or two afterward Geoffrey came to Peckham and mounted with Sonia to Fardetti's rooms, where the old man embraced him tenderly and expressed his joy in the exuberant foreign way. Geoffrey received the welcome with an Englishman's laughing embarrassment. Perhaps the only fault that Angelo Fardetti could find in the beloved pupil was his uncompromising English manner and appearance. His well-set figure and crisp, short fair hair and fair mustache did not sufficiently express him as a great musician. Angelo had to content himself with the lad's eyes—musician's eyes, as he said, very bright, arresting, dark blue, with depths like sapphires, in which lay strange thoughts and human laughter.

"I've only run in, dear old *maestro*, to pass the time of day with you, and to give you a ticket for my Queen's Hall show. You'll come, won't you?"

"He asks if I will come! I would get out of my coffin and walk through the streets!"

"I think you'll be pleased," said Geoffrey. "I've been goodness knows how long over it, and I've put into it all I know. If it doesn't come off, I'll——"

He paused.

"You will commit no rashness," cried the old man in alarm.

"I will. I'll marry Sonia the very next day!"

There was laughing talk, and the three spent a happy little quarter of an hour. But Geoffrey went away without giving either of the others an inkling of the nature of his famous symphony. It was Geoffrey's way.

The fateful afternoon arrived. Angelo Fardetti, sitting in the stalls of the Queen's Hall with Sonia and her parents, looked round the great auditorium and thrilled with pleasure at seeing it full. London had thronged to hear the first performance of his beloved's symphony. As a matter of fact, London had also come to hear the wonderful orchestra give Tchaikowsky's Fourth Symphony, and to hear Lembrich play the violin and Carli sing, which they did once in a blue moon at a symphony concert. But in the old man's eyes, these ineffectual fires paled before Geoffrey's genius. So great was his suspense and agitation that he could pay but scant attention to the first two items on the program. It seemed almost like unmeaning music, far away.

During the interval before the Symphony in E flat, his thin hand found Sonia's and held it tight, and she returned the pressure. She, too, was sick with anxiety. The great orchestra, tier upon tier, was a-flutter with the performers scrambling into their places, and with leaves of scores being turned over, and with a myriad moving bows. Then all having settled into the order of a vast machine, Geoffrey appeared at the conductor's stand. Comforting applause greeted him. Was he not the rising hope of English music? Many others beside those four to whom he was dear, and the mother and father who sat a little way in front of them, felt the same nervous apprehension. The future of English music was at stake. Would it be yet one more disappointment and disillusion, or would it rank the young English composer with the immortals? Geoffrey bowed smilingly at the audience, turned and with his baton gave the signal to begin.

Although only a few years have passed since that memorable first performance, the modestly named Symphony in E flat is now famous and Geoffrey Chase is a great man the wide world over. To every lover of music the symphony is familiar. But only those who were present at the Queen's Hall on that late October afternoon can realise the wild rapture of enthusiasm with which the symphony was greeted. It answered all longings, solved all mysteries. It interpreted, for all who had ears to hear, the fairy dew of love, the burning depths of passion, sorrow and death, and the eternal Triumph of Life. Intensely modern and faultless in technique, it was new, unexpected, individual, unrelated to any school.

The scene was one of raging tumult; but there was one human being who did not applaud, and that was the old musician, forgotten of the world, Angelo Fardetti. He had fainted.

All through the piece, he had sat, bolt upright, his nerves strung to breaking-point, his dark cheeks growing greyer and greyer, and the stare in his eyes growing more and more strange, and the grip on the girl's hand growing more and more vice-like, until she, for sheer agony, had to free herself. And none concerned themselves about him; not even Sonia, for she was enwrapped in the soul of her lover's music. And even between the movements, her heart was too full for speech or thought, and when she looked at the old man, she saw him smile wanly and nod his head as one who, like herself, was speechless with emotion. In the end the storm burst. She rose with the shouting, clapping, hand- and handkerchief-waving house, and suddenly, missing him from her side, glanced around and saw him huddled up unconscious in his stall.

The noise and movement were so great that few noticed the long lean old figure being carried out of the hall by one of the side doors fortunately near. In the vestibule, attended by the good Anton and his wife and Sonia, and a commissionaire, he recovered. When he could speak, he looked around and said:

"I am a silly old fellow. I am sorry I have spoiled your happiness. I think I must be too old for happiness, for this is how it has treated me."

There was much discussion between his friends as to what should be done, but good Mrs. Kirilov, once girlishly plump, when Angelo had first known her, now florid and fat and motherly, had her way, and, leaving Anton and Sonia to see the hero of the afternoon, if they could, drove off in a cab to Peckham with the over-wrought old man and put him to bed and gave him homely remedies, invalid food and drink, and commanded him to sleep till morning.

But Angelo Fardetti disobeyed her. For Sonia, although she had found him meekly between the sheets when she went up to see him that evening, heard him later, as she was going to bed—his sitting-room was immediately above her—playing over, on muted strings, various themes of Geoffrey's symphony. At last, she went up to his room and put her head in at the door, and saw him, a lank, dilapidated figure in an old, old dressing-gown, fiddle, and bow in hand.

"Oh! oh!" she rated. "You are a naughty, naughty old dear. Go to bed at once."

He smiled like a guilty but spoiled child. "I will go," said he.

In the morning she herself took up his simple breakfast and all the newspapers folded at the page on which the notices of the concert were printed. The Press was unanimous in acclamation of the great genius that had raised English music to the spheres. She sat at the foot of the bed and read to him while he sipped his coffee and munched his roll, and, absorbed in her own tremendous happiness, was content to feel the glow of the old man's sympathy. There was little to be said save exclamatory pæans, so overwhelming was the triumph. Tears streamed down his lined cheeks, and between the tears there shone the light of a strange gladness in his eyes. Presently Sonia left him and went about her household duties. An hour or so afterward she caught the sound of his piano; again he was recalling bits of the great symphony, and she marveled at his musical memory. Then about half-past eleven she saw him leave the house and stride away, his head in the air, his bent shoulders curiously erect.

Soon came the clatter of a cab stopping at the front door, and Geoffrey Chase, for whom she had been watching from her window, leaped out upon the pavement. She ran down and admitted him. He caught her in his arms and they stood clinging in a long embrace.

"It's too wonderful to talk about," she whispered.

"Then don't let us talk about it," he laughed.

"As if we could help it! I can think of nothing else."

"I can—you," said he, and kissed her again.

Now, in spite of the spaciousness of the house in Formosa Terrace, it had only two reception-rooms, as the house-agents grandiloquently term them, and these, dining-room and drawing-room, were respectively occupied by Anton and Mrs. Kirilov engaged in their morning lessons. The passage where the young people stood was no fit place for lovers' meetings.

"Let us go up to the *maestro's*. He's out," said Sonia.

They did as they had often done in like circumstances. Indeed, the old man, before now, had given up his sitting-room to them, feigning an unconquerable desire to walk abroad. Were they not his children, dearer to him than anyone else in the world? So it was natural that they should make themselves at

home in his tiny den. They sat and talked of the great victory, of the playing of the orchestra, of passages that he might
take slower or quicker next time, of the ovation, of the moun-
tain of congratulatory telegrams and letters that blocked up his
rooms. They talked of Angelo Fardetti and his deep emotion and
his pride. And they talked of the future, of their marriage which
was to take place very soon. She suggested postponement.

"I want you to be quite sure. This must make a difference."

"Difference!" he cried indignantly.

She waved him off and sat on the music-stool by the piano.

"I must speak sensibly. You are one of the great ones of the
musical world, one of the great ones of the world itself. You will
go on and on. You will have all sorts of honours heaped on you.
You will go about among lords and ladies, what is called Society
—oh, I know, you'll not be able to help it. And all the time I remain what I am, just a poor little common girl, a member of a
twopenny-halfpenny ladies' band. I'd rather you regretted having taken up with me before than after. So we ought to put it off."

He answered her as a good man who loves deeply can only
answer. Her heart was convinced; but she turned her head aside
and thought of further argument. Her eye fell on some music
open on the rest, and mechanically, with a musician's instinct,
she fingered a few bars. The strange familiarity of the theme
startled her out of preoccupation. She continued the treble,
and suddenly with a cold shiver of wonder, crashed down both
hands and played on.

Geoffrey strode up to her.

"What's that you're playing?"

She pointed hastily to the score. He bent over and stared at
the faded manuscript.

"Why, good God!" he cried, "it's my symphony."

She stopped, swung round and faced him with fear in her eyes.

"Yes. It's your symphony."

He took the thick manuscript from the rest and looked at the brown-paper cover. On it was written:

"The Song of Life. A Sonata by Angelo Fardetti. September 1878."

There was an amazed silence. Then, in a queer accusing voice, Sonia cried out:

"Geoffrey, what have you done?"

"Heaven knows, but I've never known of this before. My God! Open the thing somewhere else and see."

So Sonia opened the manuscript at random and played, and again it was an echo of Geoffrey's symphony. He sank on a chair like a man crushed by an overwhelming fatality and held his head in his hands.

"I oughtn't to have done it," he groaned. "But it was more than me. The thing overmastered me, it haunted me so that I couldn't sleep, and the more it haunted me the more it became my own, my very own. It was too big to lose."

Sonia held him with scared eyes.

"What are you talking of?" she asked.

"The way I came to write the Symphony. It's like a nightmare." He rose. "A couple of years ago," said he, "I bought a bundle of old music at a second-hand shop. It contained a collection of eighteenth-century stuff that I wanted. I took the whole lot, and ongoing through it, found a clump of old, discolored manuscript partly in faded brown ink, partly in pencil. It was mostly rough notes. I tried it out of curiosity. The composition was feeble and the orchestration childish—I thought it the work of some dead and forgotten amateur—but it was crammed full of ideas, crammed full of beauty. I began tinkering it about, to amuse myself. The more I worked on it the more it fascinated me. It became an obsession. Then I pitched the old score away and started it on my own."

"The *maestro* sold a lot of old music about that time," said Sonia.

The young man threw up his hands. "It's a fatality, an awful fatality. My God," he cried, "to think that I of all men should have stolen Angelo Fardetti's music!"

"No wonder he fainted yesterday," said Sonia.

It was a catastrophe. Both regarded it in remorseful silence. Sonia said at last:

"You'll have to explain."

"Of course, of course. But what must the dear old fellow be thinking of me? What else but that I've got a hold of this surreptitiously, while he was out of the room? What else but that I'm a mean thief?"

"He loves you, dear, enough to forgive you anything."

"It's the Unforgivable Sin. I'm wiped out. I cease to exist as an honest man. But I had no idea," he cried, with the instinct of self-defence, "that I had come so near him. I thought I had just got a theme here and there. I thought I had recast all the odds and ends according to my own scheme." He ran his eye over a page or two of the score. "Yes, this is practically the same as the old rough notes. But there was a lot, of course, I couldn't use. Look at that, for instance." He indicated a passage.

"I can't read it like you," said Sonia. "I must play it."

She turned again to the piano, and played the thin, uninspired music that had no relation to the Symphony in E flat, and her eyes filled with tears as she remembered poignantly what the old man had told her of his Song of Life. She went on and on until the music quickened into one of the familiar themes; and the tears fell, for she knew how poorly it was treated.

And then the door burst open. Sonia stopped dead in the middle of a bar, and they both turned round to find Angelo Fardetti standing on the threshold.

"Ah, no!" he cried, waving his thin hands. "Put that away. I did not know I had left it out. You must not play that. Ah, my son! my son!"

He rushed forward and clasped Geoffrey in his arms, and kissed him on the cheek, and murmured foolish, broken words.

"You have seen it. You have seen the miracle. The miracle of the good God. Oh, I am happy! My son, my son! I am the happiest of old men. Ah!" He shook him tremulously by both shoulders, and looked at him with a magical light in his old eyes. "You are really what our dear Anton calls a prodigy. I have thought and you have executed. Santa Maria!" he cried, raising hands and eyes to heaven. "I thank you for this miracle that has been done!"

He turned away. Geoffrey, in blank bewilderment, made a step forward.

"*Maestro*, I never knew——"

But Sonia, knowledge dawning in her face, clapped her hand over his mouth—and he read her conjecture in his eyes, and drew a great breath. The old man came again and laughed and cried and wrung his hand, and poured out his joy and wonder into the amazed ears of the conscience-stricken young musician. The floodgates of speech were loosened.

"You see what you have done, *figlio mio*. You see the miracle. This—this poor rubbish is of me, Angelo Fardetti. On it I spent my life, my blood, my tears, and it is a thing of nothing, nothing. It is wind and noise; but by the miracle of God I breathed it into your spirit and it grew—and it grew into all that I dreamed—all

23

that I dreamed and could not express. It is my Song of Life sung as I could have sung it if I had been a great genius like you. And you have taken my song from my soul, from my heart, and all the sublime harmonies that could get no farther than this dull head you have put down in immortal music."

He went on exalted, and Sonia and Geoffrey stood pale and silent. To undeceive him was impossible.

"You see it is a miracle?" he asked.

"Yes," replied Geoffrey in a low voice.

"You never saw this before. Ha! ha!" he laughed delightedly. "Not a human soul has seen it or heard it. I kept it locked up there, in my little strong-box. And it was there all the time I was teaching you. And you never suspected."

"No, *maestro*, I did not," said the young man truthfully.

"Now, when did you begin to think of it? How did it come to you—my Song of Life? Did it sing in your brain while you were here and my brain was guiding yours, and then gather form and shape all through the long years?"

"Yes," said Geoffrey. "That was how it came about."

Angelo took Sonia's plump cheeks between his hands and smiled. "Now you understand, my little Sonia, why I was so foolish yesterday. It was emotion, such emotion as a man has never felt before in the world. And now you know why I could not speak this morning. I thought of the letter you showed me. He confessed that old Angelo Fardetti had inspired him, but he did not know how. I know. The little spark flew from the soul of Angelo Fardetti into his soul, and it became a Divine Fire. And my Song of Life is true. The symphony was born in me—it died in me—it is re-born so gloriously in him. The seed is imperishable. It is eternal."

He broke away, laughing through a little sob, and stood by

the window, once more gazing unseeingly at the opposite villas of Formosa Terrace. Geoffrey went up to him and fell on his knees—it was a most un-English thing to do—and took the old hand very reverently.

"*Padre mio*," said he.

"Yes, it is true. I am your father," said the old man in Italian, "and we are bound together by more than human ties." He laid his hand on the young man's head. "May all the blessings of God be upon you."

Geoffrey rose, the humblest man in England. Angelo passed his hand across his forehead, but his face bore a beautiful smile.

"I feel so happy," said he. "So happy that it is terrible. And I feel so strange. And my heart is full. If you will forgive me, I will lie down for a little." He sank on the horse-hair sofa and smiled up in the face of the young man. "And my head is full of the *andante* movement that I could never write, and you have made it like the harmonies before the Throne of God. Sit down at the piano and play it for me, my son."

So Geoffrey took his seat at the piano, and played, and as he played, he lost himself in his music. And Sonia crept near and stood by him in a dream while the wonderful story of the passing of human things was told. When the sound of the last chords had died away she put her arms round Geoffrey's neck and laid her cheek against his. For a while time stood still. Then they turned and saw the old man sleeping peacefully. She whispered a word, he rose, and they began to tiptoe out of the room. But suddenly instinct caused Sonia to turn her head again. She stopped and gripped Geoffrey's hand. She caught a choking breath.

"Is he asleep?"

They went back and bent over him. He was dead.

Angelo Fardetti had died of a happiness too great for mortal man. To which one of us in a hundred million is it given to behold the utter realisation of his life's dream?

LADIES IN LAVENDER

I

As soon as the sun rose out of the sea its light streamed through a white-curtained casement window into the whitest and most spotless room you can imagine. It shone upon two little white beds, separated by the width of the floor covered with straw-coloured matting; on white garments neatly folded which lay on white chairs by the side of each bed; on a white enamelled bedroom suite; on the one picture (over the mantel-piece) which adorned the white walls, the enlarged photograph of a white-whiskered, elderly gentleman in naval uniform; and on the white, placid faces of the sleepers.

It awakened Miss Ursula Widdington, who sat up in bed, greeted it with a smile, and forthwith aroused her sister.

"Janet, here's the sun."

Miss Widdington awoke and smiled too.

Now to awake at daybreak with a smile and childlike delight at the sun when you are over forty-five is a sign of an unruffled conscience and a sweet disposition.

"The first glimpse of it for a week," said Miss Widdington.

"Isn't it strange," said Miss Ursula, "that when we went to sleep the storm was still raging?"

"And now—the sea hasn't gone down yet. Listen."

"The tide's coming in. Let us go out and look at it," cried Miss Ursula, delicately getting out of bed.

"You're so impulsive, Ursula," said Miss Widdington.

She was forty-eight, and three years older than her sister. She could, therefore, smile indulgently at the impetuosity of youth. But she rose and dressed, and presently the two ladies stole out of the silent house.

They had lived there for many years, perched on top of a projecting cliff on the Cornish coast, midway between sea and sky, like two fairy princesses in an enchanted bit of the world's end, who had grown grey with waiting for the prince who never came. Theirs was the only house on the wind-swept height. Below in the bay on the right of their small headland nestled the tiny fishing village of Trevannic; below, sheer down to the left, lay a little sandy cove, accessible farther on by a narrow gorge that split the majestic stretch of bastioned cliffs. To that little stone weatherbeaten house their father, the white-whiskered gentleman of the portrait, had brought them quite young when he had retired from the navy with a pension and a grievance— an ungrateful country had not made him an admiral—and there, after his death, they continued to lead their remote and gentle lives, untouched by the happenings of the great world.

The salt-laden wind buffeted them, dashed strands of hair stingingly across their faces and swirled their skirts around them as they leaned over the stout stone parapet their father had built along the edge of the cliff, and drank in the beauty of the morning. The eastern sky was clear of clouds and the eastern sea tossed a fierce silver under the sun and gradually deepened into frosted green, which changed in the west into the deep ocean blue; and the Atlantic heaved and sobbed after its turmoil of the day before. Miss Ursula pointed to the gilt-edged clouds in the west and likened them to angels' thrones, which was a pretty conceit. Miss Widdington derived a suggestion of Pentecostal flames from the golden flashes of the sea-gulls' wings. Then she referred to the appetite they would have for breakfast. To this last observation Miss Ursula did not reply, as she was leaning over the parapet intent on something in the cove below.

Presently she clutched her sister's arm.

"Janet, look down there—that black thing—what is it?"

Miss Widdington's gaze followed the pointing finger.

At the foot of the rocks that edged the gorge sprawled a thing checkered black and white.

"I do believe it's a man!"

"A drowned man! Oh, poor fellow! Oh, Janet, how dreadful!"

She turned brown, compassionate eyes on her sister, who continued to peer keenly at the helpless figure below.

"Do you think he's dead, Janet?"

"The sensible thing would be to go down and see," replied Miss Widdington.

It was by no means the first dead man cast up by the waves that they had stumbled upon during their long sojourn on this wild coast, where wrecks and founderings and loss of men's lives at sea were commonplace happenings. They were dealing with the sadly familiar; and though their gentle hearts throbbed hard as they made for the gorge and sped quickly down the ragged, rocky path, they set about their task as a matter of course.

Miss Ursula reached the sand first, and walked over to the body which lay on a low shelf of rock. Then she turned with a glad cry.

"Janet. He's alive. He's moaning. Come quickly." And, as Janet joined her: "Did you ever see such a beautiful face in your life?"

"We should have brought some brandy," said Miss Widdington.

But, as she bent over the unconscious form, a foolish moisture gathered in her eyes which had nothing to do with forgetfulness of alcohol. For indeed there lay sprawling anyhow in catlike grace beneath them the most romantic figure of a youth that the sight of maiden ladies ever rested on. He had long black hair, a perfectly chiselled face, a preposterously feminine mouth which, partly open, showed white young teeth, and the most delicate, long-fingered hands in the world. Miss Ursula murmured that he was like a young Greek god. Miss Widdington sighed. The fellow was ridiculous. He was also dank with sea water, and moaned as if he were in pain. But as gazing wrapt in wonder and admiration at young Greek gods is not much good to them when they are half-drowned, Miss Widdington despatched her sister in search of help.

"The tide is still low enough for you to get round the cliff to the village. Mrs. Pendered will give you some brandy, and her husband and Luke will bring a stretcher. You might also send Joe Gullow on his bicycle for Dr. Mead."

Miss Widdington, as behoved one who has the charge of an orphaned younger sister, did not allow the sentimental to weaken the practical. Miss Ursula, though she would have preferred to stay by the side of the beautiful youth, was docile, and went forthwith on her errand. Miss Widdington, left alone with him, rolled up her jacket and pillowed his head on it, brought his limbs into an attitude suggestive of comfort, and tried by chafing to restore him to animation. Being unsuccessful in this, she at last desisted, and sat on the rocks nearby and wondered who on earth he was and were in the world he came from. His garments consisted in a nondescript pair of trousers and a flannel shirt with a collar, which was fastened at the neck, not by button or stud, but by a tasselled cord; and he was barefoot. Miss Widdington glanced modestly at his feet, which were shapely; and the soles were soft and pink like the palms of his hands. Now, had he been the coarsest and most callosity-stricken shell-back half-alive, Janet Widdington would have tended him with the same devotion; but the lingering though unoffending Eve in her rejoiced that hands and feet betokened gentler avocations than that of sailor or fisherman. And why? Heaven knows, save that the stranded creature had a pretty face and that his long black hair was flung over his forehead in a most interesting manner. She wished he would open his eyes. But as he kept them shut and gave no sign of returning consciousness, she sat there waiting patiently; in front of her the rough, sun-kissed Atlantic, at her feet the semicircular patch of golden sand, behind her the sheer white cliffs, and by her side on the slab of rock this good-looking piece of jetsam.

At length Miss Ursula appeared round the corner of the headland, followed by Jan Pendered and his son Luke carrying a stretcher. While Miss Widdington administered brandy without any obvious result, the men looked at the castaway, scratched their heads, and guessed him to be a foreigner; but how he managed to be there alone with never a bit of wreckage to supply a clue surpassed their powers of imagination. In lifting him the right foot hung down through the trouser-leg, and his ankle was seen to be horribly black and swollen. Old Jan examined it carefully.

"Broken," said he.

"Oh, poor boy, that's why he's moaning so," cried the compassionate Miss Ursula.

The men grasped the handles of the stretcher.

"I'd better take him home to my old woman," said Jan Pendered thoughtfully.

"He can have my bed, father," said Luke.

Miss Widdington looked at Miss Ursula and Miss Ursula looked at Miss Widdington, and the eyes of each lady were wistful. Then Miss Widdington spoke.

"You can carry him up to the house, Pendered. We have a comfortable spare room, and Dorcas will help us to look after him."

The men obeyed, for in Trevannic Miss Widdington's gentle word was law.

II

It was early afternoon. Miss Widdington had retired to take her customary after-luncheon siesta, an indulgence permitted to her seniority, but not granted, except on rare occasions, to the young. Miss Ursula, therefore, kept watch in the sick chamber, just such a little white spotless room as their own, but containing only one little white bed in which the youth lay dry and warm and comfortably asleep. He was exhausted from cold and exposure, said the doctor who had driven in from St. Madoc, eight miles off, and his ankle was broken. The doctor had done what was necessary, had swathed him in one of old Dorcas's flannel nightgowns, and had departed. Miss Ursula had the patient all to herself. A bright fire burned in the grate, and the strong Atlantic breeze came in through the open window where she sat, her knitting in her hand. Now and then she glanced at the sleeper, longing, in a most feminine manner, for him to awake and render an account of himself. Miss Ursula's heart fluttered mildly. For beautiful youths, baffling curiosity, are not washed up alive by the sea at an old maid's feet every day in the week. It was indeed an adventure, a bit of a fairy tale suddenly gleaming and dancing in the grey atmosphere of an eventful life. She glanced at him again, and wondered whether he had a mother. Presently Dorcas came in, stout and matronly, and cast a maternal eye on the boy and smoothed his pillow. She had sons herself, and two of them had been claimed by the pitiless sea.

"It's lucky I had a sensible nightgown to give him," she remarked. "If we had had only the flimsy things that you and Miss Janet wear——"

"Sh!" said Miss Ursula, colouring faintly; "he might hear you."

Dorcas laughed and went out. Miss Ursula's needles clicked rapidly. When she glanced at the bed again she became conscious of two great dark eyes regarding her in utter wonder. She rose quickly and went over to the bed.

"Don't be afraid," she said, though what there was to terrify him in her mild demeanour and the spotless room she could not have explained; "don't be afraid, you're among friends."

He murmured some words which she did not catch.

"What do you say?" she asked sweetly.

He repeated them in a stronger voice. Then she realised that he spoke in a foreign tongue. A queer dismay filled her.

"Don't you speak English?"

He looked at her for a moment, puzzled. Then the echo of the last word seemed to reach his intelligence. He shook his head. A memory rose from schoolgirl days.

"*Parlez-vous français?*" she faltered; and when he shook his head again she almost felt relieved. Then he began to talk, regarding her earnestly, as if seeking by his mere intentness to make her understand. But it was a strange language which she had not heard before.

In one mighty effort Miss Ursula gathered together her whole stock of German.

"*Sprechen Sie deutsch?*"

"*Ach ja! Einige Worte,*" he replied, and his face lit up with a smile so radiant that Miss Ursula wondered how Providence could have neglected to inspire a being so beautiful with a knowledge of the English language, "*Ich kann mich auf deutsch verständlich machen, aber ich bin polnisch.*"

But not a word of the halting sentence could Miss Ursula make out; even the last was swallowed up in guttural unintelligibility. She only recognised the speech as German and different from that which he used at first, and which seemed to be his native tongue.

"Oh, dear, I must give it up," she sighed.

The patient moved slightly and uttered a sudden cry of pain. It occurred to Miss Ursula that he had not had time to realise the fractured ankle. That he realised it now was obvious, for he lay back with closed eyes and white lips until the spasm had passed. After that Miss Ursula did her best to explain in pantomime what had happened. She made a gesture of swimming, then laid her cheek on her hand and simulated fainting, acted her discovery of his body on the beach, broke a wooden match in two and pointed to his ankle, exhibited the medicine bottles by the bedside, smoothed his pillow, and smiled so as to assure him of kind treatment. He understood, more or less, murmured thanks in his own language, took her hand, and to her English woman's astonishment, pressed it to his lips. Miss Widdington, entering softly, found the pair in this romantic situation.

When it dawned on him a while later that he owed his deliverance equally to both of the gentle ladies, he kissed Miss Widdington's hand too. Whereupon Miss Ursula coloured and turned away. She did not like to see him kiss her sister's hand. Why, she could not tell, but she felt as if she had received a tiny stab in the heart.

III

Providence has showered many blessings on Trevannic, but among them is not the gift of tongues. Dr. Mead, who came over every day from St. Madoc, knew less German than the ladies. It was impossible to communicate with the boy except by signs. Old Jan Pendered, who had served in the navy in the China seas, felt confident that he could make him understand, and tried him with pidgin-English. But the youth only smiled sweetly and shook hands with him, whereupon old Jan scratched his head and acknowledged himself jiggered. To Miss Widdington, at last, came the inspiration that the oft-repeated word *"Polnisch"* meant Polish.

"You come from Poland?"

"Aus Polen, ya," laughed the boy.

"Kosciusko," murmured Miss Ursula.

He laughed again, delighted, and looked at her eagerly for more; but there Miss Ursula's conversation about Poland ended. If the discovery of his nationality lay to the credit of her sister, she it was who found out his name, Andrea Marowski, and taught him to say: "Miss Ursula." She also taught him the English names of the various objects around him. And here the innocent rivalry of the two ladies began to take definite form. Miss Widdington, without taking counsel of Miss Ursula, borrowed an old Otto's German grammar from the girls' school at St. Madoc, and, by means of patient research, put to him such questions as: "Have you a mother?" "How old are you?" and, collating his written replies with the information vouchsafed by the grammar, succeeded in discovering, among other biographical facts, that he was alone in the world, save for an old uncle who lived in Cracow, and that he was twenty years of age. So that when Miss Ursula boasted that she had taught him to say: "Good morning. How do you do?" Miss Widdington could cry with an air of triumph: "He told me that he doesn't suffer from toothache."

It was one of the curious features of the ministrations which they afforded Mr. Andrea Marowski alternately, that Miss Ursula would have nothing whatever to do with Otto's German grammar and Miss Widdington scorned the use of English and made as little use of sign language as possible.

"I don't think it becoming, Ursula," she said, "to indicate hunger by opening your mouth and rubbing the front of your waist, like a cannibal."

Miss Ursula accepted the rebuke meekly, for she never returned a pert answer to her senior; but reflecting that Janet's disapproval might possibly arise from her want of skill in the art of pantomime, she went away comforted and continued her unbecoming practices. The conversations, however, that the ladies, each in her own way, managed to have with the invalid, were sadly limited in scope. No means that they could devise could bring them enlightenment on many interesting points. Who he was, whether noble or peasant, how he came to be lying like a jellyfish on the slab of rock in their cove, coatless and barefoot, remained as great a puzzle as ever. Of course he informed them, especially the grammar-equipped Miss Widdington, over and over again in his execrable German; but they grew no wiser, and at last they abandoned in despair their attempts to solve these mysteries. They contented themselves with the actual, which indeed was enough to absorb their simple minds. There he was cast up by the sea or fallen from the moon, young, gay, and helpless, a veritable gift of the gods. The very mystery of his adventure invested him with a curious charm; and then the prodigious appetite with which he began to devour fish and eggs and chickens formed of itself a joy hitherto undreamed of in their philosophy.

"When he gets up he must have some clothes," said Miss Widdington.

Miss Ursula agreed; but did not say that she was knitting him socks in secret. Andrea's interest in the progress of these garments was one of her chief delights.

"There's the trunk upstairs with our dear father's things," said Miss Widdington with more diffidence than usual. "They are so sacred to us that I was wondering——

"Our dear father would be the first to wish it," said Miss Ursula.

"It's a Christian's duty to clothe the naked," said Miss Widdington.

"And so we must clothe him in what we've got," said Miss Ursula. Then with a slight flush she added: "It's so many years since our great loss that I've almost forgotten what a man wears."

"I haven't," said Miss Widdington. "I think I ought to tell you, Ursula," she continued, after pausing to put sugar and milk into the cup of tea which she handed to her sister—they were at the breakfast table, at the head of which she formally presided, as she had done since her emancipation from the schoolroom —"I think I ought to tell you that I have decided to devote my twenty-five pounds to buying him an outfit. Our dear father's things can only be a makeshift—and the poor boy hasn't a penny in the pockets he came ashore in."

Now, some three years before, an aunt had bequeathed Miss Widdington a tiny legacy, the disposal of which had been a continuous subject of grave discussion between the sisters. She always alluded to it as "my twenty-five pounds."

"Is that quite fair, dear?" said Miss Ursula impulsively.

"Fair? Do you mind explaining?"

Miss Ursula regretted her impetuosity. "Don't you think, dear Janet," she said with some nervousness, "that it would lay him under too great an obligation to you personally? I should prefer to take the money out of our joint income. We both are responsible for him and," she added with a timid smile, "I found him first."

"I don't see what that has to do with it," Miss Widdington retorted with a quite unusual touch of acidity. "But if you feel strongly about it, I am willing to withdraw my five-and-twenty pounds."

"You're not angry with me, Janet?"

"Angry? Of course not," Miss Widdington replied freezingly. "Don't be silly. And why aren't you eating your bacon?"

This was the first shadow of dissension that had arisen between them since their childhood. On the way to the sick-room, Miss Ursula shed a few tears over Janet's hectoring ways, and Miss Widdington, in pursuit of her housekeeping duties, made Dorcas the scapegoat for Ursula's unreasonableness. Before luncheon time they kissed with mutual apologies; but the spirit of rivalry was by no means quenched.

IV

One afternoon Miss Janet had an inspiration.

"If I played the piano in the drawing-room with the windows open you could hear it in the spare room quite plainly."

"If you think it would disturb Mr. Andrea," said Miss Ursula, "you might shut the windows."

"I was proposing to offer him a distraction, dear," said Miss Widdington. "These foreign gentlemen are generally fond of music."

Miss Ursula could raise no objection, but her heart sank. She could not play the piano.

She took her seat cheerfully, however, by the bed, which had been wheeled up to the window, so that the patient could look out on the glory of sky and sea, took her knitting from a drawer and began to turn the heel of one of the sacred socks. Andrea watched her lazily and contentedly. Perhaps he had never seen two such soft-treaded, soft-fingered ladies in lavender in his life. He often tried to give some expression to his gratitude, and the hand-kissing had become a thrice daily custom. For Miss Widdington he had written the word "Engel," which the vocabulary at the end of Otto's German grammar rendered as "Angel"; whereat she had blushed quite prettily. For Miss Ursula he had drawn, very badly, but still unmistakably, the picture of a winged denizen of Paradise, and she, too, had treasured the compliment; she also treasured the drawing. Now, Miss Ursula held up the knitting, which began distinctly to indicate the shape of a sock, and smiled. Andrea smiled, too, and blew her a kiss with his fingers. He had many graceful foreign gestures. The doctor, who was a plain, bullet-headed Briton, disapproved of Andrea and expressed to Dorcas his opinion that the next things to be washed ashore would be the young man's monkey and organ. This was sheer prejudice, for Andrea's manners were unexceptionable, and his smile, in the eyes of his hostesses, the most attractive thing in the world.

"Heel," said Miss Ursula.

"'Eel," repeated Andrea.

"Wool," said Miss Ursula.

"Vool," said Andrea.

"No—wo-o," said Miss Ursula, puffing out her lips so as to accentuate the "w."

"Wo-o," said Andrea, doing the same. And then they both burst out laughing. They were enjoying themselves mightily.

Then, from the drawing-room below, came the tinkling sound of the old untuned piano which had remained unopened for many years. It was the "Spring Song" of Mendelssohn, played, schoolgirl fashion, with uncertain fingers that now and then struck false notes. The light died away from Andrea's face, and he looked inquiringly, if not wonderingly, at Miss Ursula. She smiled encouragement, pointed first at the floor, and then at him, thereby indicating that the music was for his benefit. For awhile he remained quite patient. At last he clapped his hands on his ears, and his features distorted with pain, cried out:

"Nein, nein, nein, das lieb' ich nicht! Es ist hässlich!"

In eager pantomime he besought her to stop the entertainment. Miss Ursula went downstairs, hating to hurt her sister's feelings, yet unable to crush a wicked, unregenerate feeling of pleasure.

"I am so sorry, dear Janet," she said, laying her hand on her sister's arm, "but he doesn't like music. It's astonishing, his dislike. It makes him quite violent."

Miss Widdington ceased playing and accompanied her sister upstairs. Andrea, with an expressive shrug of the shoulders, reached out his two hands to the musician and, taking hers, kissed her finger-tips. Miss Widdington consulted Otto.

"Lieben Sie nicht Musik?"

"Ja wohl," he cried, and laughing, played an imaginary fiddle.

"He *does* like music," cried Miss Widdington. "How can you make such silly mistakes, Ursula? Only he prefers the violin."

Miss Ursula grew downcast for a moment; then she brightened. A brilliant idea occurred to her.

"Adam Penruddocke. He has a fiddle. We can ask him to come up after tea and play to us."

She reassured Andrea in her queer sign-language, and later in the afternoon Adam Penruddocke, a sheepish giant of a fisherman, was shown into the room. He bowed to the ladies, shook the long white hand proffered him by the beautiful youth, tuned up, and played "The Carnival of Venice" from start to finish. Andrea regarded him with mischievous, laughing eyes, and at the end he applauded vigorously.

Miss Widdington turned to her sister.

"I knew he liked music," she said.

"Shall I play something else, sir?" asked Penruddocke.

Andrea, guessing his meaning, beckoned him to approach the bed, and took the violin and bow from his hands. He looked at the instrument critically, smiled to himself, tuned it afresh, and with an air of intense happiness drew the bow across the strings.

"Why, he can play it!" cried Miss Ursula.

Andrea laughed and nodded, and played a bit of "The Carnival of Venice" as it ought to be played, with gaiety and mischief. Then he broke off, and after two or three tearing chords that made his hearers start, plunged into a wild czardas. The ladies looked at him in open-mouthed astonishment as the mad music such as they had never heard in their lives before filled the little room with its riot and devilry. Penruddocke stood and panted, his eyes staring out of his head. When Andrea had finished there was a bewildered silence. He nodded pleasantly at his audience, delighted at the effect he had produced. Then, with an artist's malice, he went to the other extreme of emotion. He played a sobbing folk-song, rending the heart with cries of woe and desolation and broken hopes. It clutched at the heart-strings, turning them into vibrating chords; it pierced the soul with its poignant despair; it ended in a long-drawn-out note high up in the treble, whose pain became intolerable; and the end was greeted with a sharp gasp of relief. The white lips of the ruddy giant quivered. Tears streamed down the cheeks of Miss Widdington and Miss Ursula. Again there was silence, but this time it was broken by a clear, shrill voice outside.

"Encore! Encore!"

The sisters looked at one another. Who had dared intrude at such a moment? Miss Widdington went to the window to see.

In the garden stood a young woman of independent bearing, with a palette and brushes in her hand. An easel was pitched a few yards beyond the gate. Miss Widdington regarded this young woman with marked disfavour. The girl calmly raised her eyes.

"I apologise for trespassing like this," she said, "but I simply couldn't resist coming nearer to this marvellous violin-playing —and my exclamation came out almost unconsciously."

"You are quite welcome to listen," said Miss Widdington stiffly.

"May I ask who is playing it?"

Miss Widdington almost gasped at the girl's impertinence. The latter laughed frankly.

"I ask because it seems as if it could only be one of the big, well-known people."

"It's a young friend who is staying with us," said Miss Widdington.

"I beg your pardon," said the girl. "But, you see my brother is Boris Danilof, the violinist, so I've that excuse for being interested."

"I don't think Mr. Andrea can play any more to-day," said Miss Ursula from her seat by the bed. "He's tired."

Miss Widdington repeated this information to Miss Danilof, who bade her good afternoon and withdrew to her easel.

"A most forward, objectionable girl," exclaimed Miss Widdington. "And who is Boris Danilof, I should like to know?"

If she had but understood German, Andrea could have told her. He caught at the name of the world-famous violinist and bent eagerly forward in great excitement.

"Boris Danilof? *Ist er unten?*"

"*Nicht*—I mean *Nein*," replied Miss Widdington, proud at not having to consult Otto.

Andrea sank back disappointed, on his pillow.

V

However much Miss Widdington disapproved of the young woman, and however little the sisters knew of Boris Danilof, it was obvious that they were harbouring a remarkable violinist. That even the bullet-headed doctor, who had played the double bass in his Hospital Orchestral Society and was, therefore, an authority, freely admitted. It gave the romantic youth a new and somewhat awe-inspiring value in the eyes of the ladies. He was a genius, said Miss Ursula—and her imagination became touched by the magic of the word. As he grew stronger he played more. His fame spread through the village and he gave recitals to crowded audiences—as many fisher-folk as could be squeezed into the little bedroom, and more standing in the garden below. Miss Danilof did not come again. The ladies learned that she was staying in the next village, Polwern, two or three miles off. In their joy at Andrea's recovery they forgot her existence.

Happy days came when he could rise from bed and hobble about on a crutch, attired in the quaint garments of Captain Widdington, R.N., who had died twenty years before, at the age of seventy-three. They added to his romantic appearance, giving him the air of the *jeune premier* in costume drama. There was a blue waistcoat with gilt buttons, calculated to win any feminine approval. The ladies admired him vastly. Conversation was still difficult, as Miss Ursula had succeeded in teaching him very little English, and Miss Widdington, after a desperate grapple with Otto on her own account, had given up the German language in despair. But what matters the tongue when the heart speaks? And the hearts of Miss Widdington and Miss

Ursula spoke; delicately, timidly, tremulously, in the whisper of an evening breeze, in undertones, it is true—yet they spoke all the same. The first walks on the heather of their cliff in the pure spring sunshine were rare joys. As they had done with their watches by his bedside, they took it in turns to walk with him; and each in her turn of solitude felt little pricklings of jealousy. But as each had instituted with him her own particular dainty relations and confidences—Miss Widdington more maternal, Miss Ursula more sisterly—to which his artistic nature responded involuntarily, each felt sure that she was the one who had gained his especial affection.

Thus they wove their gossamer webs of romance in the secret recesses of their souls. What they hoped for was as dim and vague as their concept of heaven, and as pure. They looked only at the near future—a circle of light encompassed by mists; but in the circle stood ever the beloved figure. They could not imagine him out of it. He would stay with them, irradiating their lives with his youth and his gaiety, playing to them his divine music, kissing their hands, until he grew quite strong and well again. And that was a long, long way off. Meanwhile life was a perpetual spring. Why should it ever end?

One afternoon they sat in the sunny garden, the ladies busy with needlework, and Andrea playing snatches of dreamy things on the violin. The dainty remains of tea stood on a table, and the young man's crutch rested against it. Presently he began to play Tschaikowsky's "Chanson Triste." Miss Ursula, looking up, saw a girl of plain face and independent bearing standing by the gate.

"Who is that, Janet?" she whispered.

Miss Janet glanced round.

"It is the impertinent young woman who was listening the other day."

Andrea followed their glances, and, perceiving a third listener, half consciously played to her. When the piece was finished the girl slowly walked away.

"I know it's wrong and unchristian like," said Miss Widdington, "but I dislike that girl intensely."

"So do I," said Miss Ursula. Then she laughed. "She looks like the wicked fairy in a story-book."

VI

The time came when he threw aside his crutch and flew, laughing, away beyond their control. This they did not mind, for he always came back and accompanied them on their wild rambles. He now resembled the ordinary young man of the day as nearly as the St. Madoc tailors and hosiers could contrive; and the astonishing fellow, with his cameo face and his hyacinthine locks, still looked picturesque.

One morning he took Pendruddocke's fiddle and went off, in high spirits, and when he returned in the late afternoon his face was flushed and a new light burned in his eyes. He explained his adventures volubly. They had a vague impression that, Orion-like, he had been playing his stringed instrument to dolphins and waves and things some miles off along the coast. To please him they said "*Ja*" at every pause in his narration, and he thought they understood. Finally he kissed their hands.

Two mornings later he started, without his fiddle, immediately after breakfast. To Miss Ursula, who accompanied him down the road to the village, he announced Polwern as his destination. Unsuspecting and happy, she bade him good-bye and lovingly watched his lithe young figure disappear behind the bounding cliff of the little bay.

Miss Olga Danilof sat reading a novel by the door of the cottage where she lodged when the beautiful youth came up. He raised his hat—she nodded.

"Well," she said in German, "have you told the funny old maids?"

"*Ach*," said he, "they are dear, gracious ladies—but I have told them."

"I've heard from my brother," she remarked, taking a letter from the book. "He trusts my judgment implicitly, as I said he would—and you are to come with me to London at once."

"To-day?"

"By the midday train."

He looked at her in amazement. "But the dear ladies——"

"You can write and explain. My brother's time is valuable—he has already put off his journey to Paris one day in order to see you."

"But I have no money," he objected weakly.

"What does that matter? I have enough for the railway ticket, and when you see Boris he will give you an advance. Oh, don't be grateful," she added in her independent way. "In the first place, we're brother artists, and in the second it's a pure matter of business. It's much better to put yourself in the hands of Boris Danilof and make a fortune in Europe than to play in a restaurant orchestra in New York; don't you think so?"

Andrea did think so, and he blessed the storm that drove the ship out of its course from Hamburg and terrified him out of his wits in his steerage quarters, so he rushed on deck in shirt and trousers, grasping a life-belt, only to be cursed one moment by a sailor and the next to be swept by a wave clean over the taffrail into the sea. He blessed the storm and he blessed the wave and he blessed the life-belt which he lost just before consciousness left him; and he blessed the jag of rock on the sandy cove against which he must have broken his ankle; and he blessed the ladies and the sun and the sea and sky and Olga Danilof and the whole of this beautiful world that had suddenly laid itself at his feet.

The village cart drew up by the door, and Miss Danilof's luggage that lay ready in the hall was lifted in.

"Come," she said. "You can ask the old maids to send on your things."

He laughed. "I have no things. I am as free as the wind."

At St. Madoc, whence he intended to send a telegram to the dear, gracious ladies, they only had just time to catch the train. He sent no telegram; and as they approached London he thought less and less about it, his mind, after the manner of youth, full of the wonder that was to be.

VII

The ladies sat down to tea. Eggs were ready to be boiled as soon as he returned. Not having lunched, he would be hungry. But he did not come. By dinner-time they grew anxious. They postponed the meal. Dorcas came into the drawing-room periodically to report deterioration of cooked viands. But they could not eat the meal alone. At last they grew terrified lest some evil should have befallen him, and Miss Widdington went in to the village and despatched Jan Pendered, and Joe Gullow on his bicycle, in search. When she returned she found Miss Ursula looking as if she had seen a ghost.

"Janet, that girl is living there."

"Where?"

"Polwern. He went there this morning."

Miss Widdington felt as if a cold hand had touched her heart, but she knew that it behoved her as the elder to dismiss her sister's fears.

"You're talking nonsense, Ursula; he has never met her."

"How do we know?" urged Miss Ursula.

"I don't consider it delicate," replied Miss Widdington, "to discuss the possibility."

They said no more, and went out and stood by the gate, waiting for their messengers. The moon rose and silvered the sea, and the sea breeze sprang up; the surf broke in a melancholy rhythm on the sands beneath.

"It sounds like the 'Chanson Triste,'" said Miss Ursula. And before them both rose the picture of the girl standing there like an Evil Fairy while Andrea played.

At last Jan Pendered appeared on the cliff. The ladies went out to meet him.

Then they learned what had happened.

In a dignified way they thanked Jan Pendered and gave him a shilling for Joe Gullow, who had brought the news. They bade him good night in clear, brave voices, and walked back very silent and upright through the garden into the house. In the drawing-room they turned to each other, and, their arms about each other's necks, they broke down utterly.

The stranger woman had come and had taken him away from them. Youth had flown magnetically to youth. They were left alone unheeded in the dry lavender of their lives.

The moonlight streamed through the white-curtained casement window into the white, spotless room. It shone on the two little white beds, on the white garments, neatly folded on white chairs, on the white-whiskered gentleman over the mantle-piece, and on the white faces of the sisters. They slept little that night. Once Miss Widdington spoke.

"Ursula, we must go to sleep and forget it all. We've been two old fools."

Miss Ursula sobbed for answer. With the dawn came a certain quietude of spirit. She rose, put on her dressing-gown, and, leaving her sister asleep, stole out on tiptoe. The window was open and the curtains were undrawn in the boy's empty room. She leaned on the sill and looked out over the sea. Sooner or later, she knew, would come a letter of explanation. She hoped Janet would not force her to read it. She no longer wanted to know whence he came, whither he was going. It were better for her, she thought, not to know. It were better for her to cherish the most beautiful thing that had ever entered her life. For all those years she had waited for the prince who never came; and he had come at last out of fairyland, cast up by the sea. She had had with him her brief season of tremulous happiness. If he had been carried on, against his will, by the strange woman into the unknown whence he had emerged, it was only the inevitable ending of such a fairy tale.

Thus wisdom came to her from the sea and sky, and made her strong. She smiled through her tears, and she, the weaker, went forth for the first time in her life to comfort and direct her sister.

STUDIES IN BLINDNESS

AN OLD-WORLD EPISODE

I

I have often thought of editing the diary (which is in my possession) of one Jeremy Wendover, of Bullingford, in the county of Berkshire, England, Gent., who departed this life in the year of grace 1758, and giving to the world a document as human as the record of Pepys and as deeply imbued with the piety of a devout Christian as the Confessions of Saint Augustine. A little emendation of an occasional ungrammatical and disjointed text—though in the main the diary is written in the scholarly, florid style of the eighteenth century; a little intelligent conjecture as to certain dates; a footnote now and then elucidating an obscure reference—and the thing would be done. It has been a great temptation, but I have resisted it. The truth is that to the casual reader the human side would seem to be so meagre, the pietistic so full. One has to seek so carefully for a few flowers of fact among a wilderness of religious and philosophical fancy —nay, more: to be so much in sympathy with the diarist as to translate the pious rhetoric into terms of mundane incident, that only to the curious student can the real life history of the man be revealed. And who in these hurrying days would give weeks of patient toil to a task so barren of immediate profit? I myself certainly would not do it; and it is a good working philosophy of life (though it has its drawbacks) not to expect others to do what you would not do yourself. It is only because the study of these yellow pages, covered with the brown, almost microscopic, pointed handwriting, has amused the odd moments of years that I have arrived at something like a comprehension of the things that mattered so much to Jeremy Wendover, and so pathetically little to any other of the sons and daughters of Adam.

How did the diary, you ask, come into my possession? I picked it up, years ago, for a franc, at a second-hand booksellers in Geneva. It had the bookplate of a long-forgotten Bishop of Sodor and Man, and an inscription on the flyleaf: "John Henderson, Calcutta, 1835." How it came into the hands of the Bishop, into those of John Henderson, how it passed thence and eventually found its way to Geneva, Heaven alone knows.

I have said that Jeremy Wendover departed this life in 1758. My authority for this statement is a lichen-covered gravestone in the churchyard of Bullingford, whither I have made many pious pilgrimages in the hope of finding more records of my obscure hero. But I have been unsuccessful. The house, however, in which he lived, described at some length in his diary, is still standing—an Early Tudor building, the residence of the maltster who owned the adjoining long, gabled malthouse, and from whom he rented it for a considerable term of years. It is situated on the river fringe of the little town, at the end of a lane running at right angles to the main street just before this loses itself in the market square.

I have stood at the front gate of the house and watched the Thames, some thirty yards away, flow between its alder-grown banks; the wide, lush meadows and cornfields beyond dotted here and there with the red roofs of farms and spreading amid the quiet greenery of oaks and chestnuts to the low-lying Oxfordshire hills; I have breathed in the peace of the evening air and I have found myself very near in spirit to Jeremy Wendover, who stood, as he notes, many and many a summer afternoon at that self-same gate, watching the selfsame scene, far away from the fever and the fret of life.

I have thought, therefore, that instead of publishing his diary I might with some degree of sympathy set forth in brief the one dramatic episode in his inglorious career.

II

The overwhelming factor in Jeremy Wendover's life was the appalling, inconceivable hideousness of his face. The refined, cultivated, pious gentleman was cursed with a visage which it would have pleased Dante to ascribe to a White Guelph whom he particularly disliked, and would have made Orcagna shudder in the midst of his dreams of shapes of hell. As a child of six, in a successful effort to rescue a baby sister, he had fallen head-foremost into a great wood fire, and when they picked him up his face "was like unto a charred log that had long smouldered." Almost the semblance of humanity had been wiped from him, and to all beholders he became a thing of horror. Men turned their heads away, women shivered and children screamed at his approach. He was a pariah, condemned from early boyhood to an awful loneliness. His parents, a certain Sir Julius Wendover, Baronet, and his wife, his elder brother and his sisters—they must have been a compassionless family—turned from him as from an evil and pestilential thing. Love never touched him with its consoling feather, and for love the poor wretch pinned his whole youth long. Human companionship, even, was denied him. He seems to have lived alone in a wing of a great house, seldom straying beyond the bounds of the park, under the tutorship of a reverend but scholarly sot who was too drunken and obese and unbuttoned to be admitted into the family circle. This fellow, one Doctor Tubbs, of St. Catherine's College,

Cambridge, seems to have shown Jeremy some semblance of affection, but chiefly while in his cups, "when," as Jeremy puts it bitterly, "he was too much like unto the beasts that perish to distinguish between me and a human being." When sober he railed at the boy for a monster, and frequently chastised him for his lack of beauty. But, in some strange way, in alternate fits of slobbering and castigating, he managed to lay the groundwork of a fine education, teaching Jeremy the classics, Italian and French, some mathematics, and the elements of philosophy and theology; he also discoursed much to him on the great world, of which, till his misfortunes came upon him, he boasted of having been a distinguished ornament; and when he had three bottles of wine inside him he told his charge very curious and instructive things indeed.

So Jeremy grew to man's estate, sensitive, shy, living in the world of books and knowing little, save at second-hand, of the ways of men and women. But with all the secrets of the birds and beasts in the far-stretching Warwickshire park he was intimately acquainted. He became part of the woodland life. Squirrels would come to him and munch their acorns on his shoulder.

"So intimate was I in this innocent community," says he, not without quiet humour, "that I have been a wet-nurse to weasels and called in as physician to a family of moles."

When Sir Julius died, Jeremy received his younger son's portion (fortunately, it was a goodly one) and was turned neck and crop out of the house by his ill-conditioned brother. Tubbs, having also suffered ignominious expulsion, persuaded him to go on the grand tour. They started. But they only got as far as Abbeville on the road to Paris, where Tubbs was struck down by an apoplexy of which he died. Up to that point the sot's company had enabled Jeremy to endure the insult, ribaldry and terror that attended his unspeakable deformity; but, left alone, he lost heart; mankind rejected him as a pack of wolves rejects a maimed cub. Stricken with shame and humiliation he crept back to England and established himself in the maltster's house at Bullingford, guided thither by no other consideration than that it had been the birthplace of the dissolute Tubbs. He took up his lonely abode there as a boy of three-and-twenty, and there he spent the long remainder of his life.

III

The great event happened in his thirty-fourth year. You may picture him as a solitary, scholarly figure living in the little Tudor house, with its mullioned windows, set in the midst of an old-world garden bright with stocks and phlox and holly-hocks and great pink roses, its southern wall generously glow-ing with purple plums. Indoors, the house was somewhat dark. The casement window of the main living-room was small and overshadowed by the heavy ivy outside. The furniture, of plain dark oak, mainly consisted of bookcases, in which were ranged the solemn, leather-covered volumes that were Jeremy's world. A great table in front of the window contained the books of the moment, the latest news-sheets from London, and the great brass-clasped volume in which he wrote his diary. In front of it stood a great straight-backed chair.

You may picture him on a late August afternoon, sitting in this chair, writing his diary by the fading light. His wig lay on the table, for the weather was close. He paused, pen in hand, and looked wistfully at the mellow eastern sky, lost in thought. Then he wrote these words:

O Lord Jesus, fill me plentifully with Thy love, which passeth the love of woman; for love of woman never will be mine, and there-fore, O Lord, I require Thy love bountifully: I yearn for love even as a weaned child. Even as a weaned child yearns for the breast of its mother, so yearn I for love.

He closed and clasped the book with a sigh, put on his wig, rose and, going into the tiny hall, opened the kitchen door and announced to his household, one ancient and incompetent crone, his intention of taking the air. Then he clapped on his old three-cornered hat and stick in hand, went out of the front gate into the light of the sunset. He stood for a while watching the deep reflections of the alders and willows in the river and the golden peace of the meadows beyond, and his heart was uplifted in thankfulness for the beauty of the earth. He was a tall, thin man, with the stoop of the scholar and, despite his rough, country-made clothes, the unmistakable air of the eighteenth-century gentleman. The setting sun shone full on the piteous medley of marred features that served him for a face.

A woman, sickle on arm, leading a toddling child, passed by with averted head. But she curtsied and said respectfully: "Good evening, your honour." The child looked at him with a cry of fear shrank into the mother's skirts. Jeremy touched his hat.

"Good evening, Mistress Blackacre. I trust your husband is recovered from his fever."

"Thanks to your honour's kindness," said the woman, her eyes always turned from him, "he is well-nigh recovered. For shame of yourself!" she added, shaking the child.

"Nay, nay," said Jeremy kindly. "'Tis not the urchin's fault that he met a bogey in broad daylight."

He strolled along the river bank, pleased at his encounter. In that little backwater of the world where he had lived secluded for ten years folks had learned to suffer him—nay, more, to respect him: and though they seldom looked him in the face their words were gentle and friendly. He could even jest at his own misfortune.

"God is good," he murmured as he walked with head bent down and hands behind his back, "and the earth is full of His goodness. Yet if He in His mercy could only give me a companion in my loneliness, as He gives to every peasant, bird and beast ____"

A sigh ended the sentence. He was young and not always able to control the squabble between sex and piety. The words had scarcely passed his lips, however, when he discerned a female figure seated on the bank, some fifty yards away. His first impulse—an impulse which the habit of years would, on ordinary occasions, have rendered imperative—was to make a wide detour round the meadows; but this evening the spirit of mild revolt took possession of him and guided his steps in the direction of the lady—for lady he perceived her to be when he drew a little nearer.

She wore a flowered muslin dress cut open at the neck, and her arms, bare to the elbows, were white and shapely. A peach-blossom of a face appeared below the mob-cap bound by a cherry-coloured ribbon, and as Jeremy came within speaking distance her dark-blue eyes were fixed on him fearlessly. Jeremy halted and looked at her, while she looked at Jeremy. His heart beat wildly. The miracle of miracles had happened—the hopeless, impossible thing that he had prayed for in rebellious hours for so many years, ever since he had realised that the world held such a thing as the joy and the blessing of woman's love. A girl looked at him smilingly, frankly in the face, without a quiver of repulsion—and a girl more dainty and beautiful than any he had seen before. Then, as he stared, transfixed like a person in a beatitude, into her eyes, something magical occurred to Jeremy. The air was filled with the sound of fairy harps of which his own tingling nerves from head to foot were the vibrating strings. Jeremy fell instantaneously in love.

"Will you tell me, sir," she said in a musical voice—the music of the spheres to Jeremy—"will you tell me how I can reach the house of Mistress Wotherspoon?"

Jeremy took off his three-cornered hat and made a sweeping bow.

"Why, surely, madam," said he, pointing with his stick; "'tis yonder red roof peeping through the trees only three hundred yards distant."

"You are a gentleman," said the girl quickly.

"My name is Jeremy Wendover, younger son of the late Sir Julius Wendover, Baronet, and now and always, madam, your very humble servant."

She smiled. Her rosy lips and pearly teeth (Jeremy's own description) filled Jeremy's head with lunatic imaginings.

"And I, sir," said she, "am Mistress Barbara Seaforth, and I came but yesterday to stay with my aunt, Mistress Wotherspoon. If I could trespass so far on your courtesy as to pray you to conduct me thither I should be vastly beholden to you."

His sudden delight at the proposition was mingled with some astonishment. She only had to walk across the open meadow to the clump of trees. He assisted her to rise and with elaborate politeness offered his arm. She made no motion, however, to take it.

"I thought I was walking in my aunt's little railed enclosure," she remarked; "but I must have passed through the gate into the open fields, and when I came to the river I was frightened and sat down and waited for someone to pass."

"Pray pardon me, madam," said Jeremy, "but I don't quite understand——"

"La, sir! how very thoughtless of me," she laughed. "I never told you. I am blind."

"Blind!" he echoed. The leaden weight of a piteous dismay fell upon him. That was why she had gazed at him so fearlessly. She had not seen him. The miracle had not happened. For a moment he lost count of the girl's sad affliction in the stress of his own bitterness. But the lifelong habit of resignation prevailed.

"Madam, I crave your pardon for not having noticed it," he said in an unsteady voice. "And I admire the fortitude wherewith you bear so grievous a burden."

"Just because I can't see is no reason for my drowning the world in my tears. We must make the best of things. And there are compensations, too," she added lightly, allowing her hand to be placed on his arm and led away. "I refer to an adventure with a young gentleman which, were I not blind, my Aunt Wotherspoon would esteem mightily unbecoming."

"Alas, madam," he said with a sigh, "there you are wrong. I am not young. I am thirty-three."

He thought it was a great age. Mistress Barbara turned up her face saucily and laughed. Evidently, she did not share his opinion. Jeremy bent a wistful gaze into the beautiful, sightless eyes, and then saw what had hitherto escaped his notice: a thin; grey film over the pupils.

"How did you know," he asked, "that I was a man, when I came up to you?"

"First by your aged, tottering footsteps, sir," she said with a pretty air of mockery, "which were not those of a young girl. And then you were standing 'twixt me and the sun, and one of my poor eyes can still distinguish light from shadow."

"How long have you suffered from this great affliction?" he asked.

"I have been going blind for two years. It is now two months since I have lost sight altogether. But please don't talk of it," she added hastily. "If you pity me I shall cry, which I hate, for I want to laugh as much as I can. I can also walk faster, sir, if it would not tire your aged limbs."

Jeremy started guiltily. She had divined his evil purpose. But who will blame him for not wishing to relinquish oversoon the delicious pressure of her little hand on his arm and to give over this blind flower of womanhood into another's charge? He replied disingenuously, without quickening his pace:

"'Tis for your sake, madam, I am walking slowly. The afternoon is warm."

"I am vastly sensible of your gallantry, sir," she retorted. "But I fear you must have practised it much on others to have arrived at this perfection."

"By heavens, madam," he cried, cut to the heart by her innocent raillery, "'tis not so. Could you but see me you would know it was not. I am a recluse, a student, a poor creature set apart from the ways of men. You are the first woman that has walked arm-in-arm with me in all my life—except in dreams. And now my dream has come true."

His voice vibrated, and when she answered hers was responsive.

"You, too, have your burden?"

"Could you but know how your touch lightens it!" said he.

She blushed to the brown hair that was visible beneath the mob-cap.

"Are we very far now from my Aunt Wotherspoon's?" she asked. Whereupon Jeremy, abashed, took refuge in the commonplace.

The open gate through which she had strayed was reached all too quickly. When she had passed through she made him a curtsey and held out her hand. He touched it with his lips as if it were sacramental bread. She avowed herself much beholden to his kindness.

"Shall I ever see you again, Mistress Barbara?" he asked in a low voice, for an old servant was hobbling down from the house to meet her.

"My Aunt Wotherspoon is bed-ridden and receives no visitors."

"But I could be of no further service to you?" pleaded Jeremy.

She hesitated and then she said demurely:

"It would be a humane action, sir, to see sometimes that this gate is shut, lest I stray through it again and drown myself in the river."

Jeremy could scarce believe his ears.

IV

This was the beginning of Jeremy's love-story. He guarded the gate like Cerberus or Saint Peter. Sometimes at dawn he would creep out of his house and tramp through the dew-filled meadows to see that it was safely shut. During the day he would do sentry-go within sight of the sacred portal, and when the flutter of a mob-cap and a flowered muslin met his eye he would advance merely to report that the owner ran no danger. And then, one day, she bade him open it, and she came forth and they walked arm-in-arm in the meadows; and this grew to be a daily custom, to the no small scandal of the neighbourhood. Very soon, Jeremy learned her simple history. She was an orphan, with a small competence of her own. Until recently she had lived in Somersetshire with her guardian; but now he was dead, and the only home she could turn to was that of her bed-ridden Aunt Wotherspoon, her sole surviving relative.

Jeremy, with a lamentable lack of universality, thanked God on his knees for His great mercy. If Mistress Wotherspoon had not been confined to her bed she would not have allowed her niece to wander at will with a notorious scarecrow over the Bullingford meadows, and if Barbara had not been blind she could not have walked happily in his company and hung trustfully on his arm. For days she was but a wonder and a wild desire. Her beauty, her laughter, her wit, her simplicity, her bravery, bewildered him. It was enough to hear the music of her voice, to feel the fragrance of her presence, to thrill at her light touch. He, Jeremy Wendover, from whose distortion all human beings, his life long, had turned shuddering away, to have this ineffable companionship! It transcended thought. At last—it was one night, as he lay awake, remembering how they had walked that afternoon, not arm-in-arm, but hand-in-hand—the amazing, dazzling glory of a possibility enveloped him. She was blind. She could never see his deformity. Had God listened to his prayer and delivered this fair and beloved woman into his keeping? He shivered all night long in an ecstasy of happiness, rose at dawn and mounted guard at Barbara's gate. But as he waited, foodless, for the thrilling sight of her, depression came and sat heavy on his shoulders until he felt that in daring to think of her in the way of marriage he was committing an abominable crime.

When she came, fresh as the morning, bareheaded, her beautiful hair done up in a club behind, into the little field, and he tried to call to her, his tongue was dry and he could utter no sound. Accidentally he dropped his stick, which clattered down the bars of the gate. She laughed. He entered the enclosure.

"I knew I should find you there," she cried, and sped toward him.

"How did you know?" he asked.

"'By the pricking of my thumb,'" she quoted gaily; and then, as he took both her outstretched hands, she drew near him and whispered: "and by the beating of my heart."

His arms folded around her and he held her tight against him, stupefied, dazed, throbbing, vainly trying to find words. At last he said huskily:

"God has sent you to be the joy and comfort of a sorely stricken man. I accept it because it is His will. I will cherish you as no man has ever cherished woman before. My love for you, my dear, is as infinite—as infinite—oh, God!"

Speech failed him. He tore his arms away from her and fell sobbing at her feet and kissed the skirts of her gown.

V

The Divine Mercy, as Jeremy puts it, thought fit to remove Aunt Wotherspoon to a happier world before the week was out; and so, within a month, Jeremy led his blind bride into the little Tudor house. And then began for him a happiness so exquisite that sometimes he was afraid to breathe lest he should disturb the enchanted air. Every germ of love and tenderness that had lain undeveloped in his nature sprang into flower. Sometimes he grew afraid lest, in loving her, he was forgetting God. But he reassured himself by a pretty sophistry. "O Lord," says he, "it is Thou only that I worship—through Thine own great gift." And indeed what more could be desired by a reasonable Deity?

Barbara, responsive, gave him her love in full. From the first she would hear nothing of his maimed visage.

"My dear," she said as they wandered one golden autumn day by the riverside, "I have made a picture of you out of your voice, the plash of water, the sunset and the summer air. 'Twas thus that my heart saw you the first evening we met. And that is more than sufficing for a poor, blind creature whom a gallant gentleman married out of charity."

"Charity!" His voice rose in indignant repudiation.

She laughed and laid her head on her shoulder.

"Ah, dear, I did but jest. I know you fell in love with my pretty doll's face. And also with a little mocking spirit of my own."

"But what made you fall in love with me?"

"Faith, Mr. Wendover," she replied, "a woman with eyes in her head has but to go whither she is driven. And so much the more a blind female like me. You led me plump into the middle of the morass; and when you came and rescued me I was silly enough to be grateful."

Under Jeremy's love her rich nature expanded day by day. She set her joyous courage and her wit to work to laugh at blindness, and to make her the practical, serviceable housewife as well as the gay companion. The ancient crone was replaced by a brisk servant and a gardener, and Jeremy enjoyed creature comforts undreamed of. And the months sped happily by. Autumn darkened into winter and winter cleared into spring, and daffodils and crocuses and primroses began to show themselves in corners of the old-world garden, and tiny gossamer garments in corners of the dark old house. Then a newer, deeper happiness enfolded them.

But there came a twilight hour when, whispering of the wonder that was to come, she suddenly began to cry softly.

"But why, why, dear?" he asked in tender astonishment.

"Only—only to think, Jeremy, that I shall never see it."

VI

One evening in April, while Jeremy was reading and Barbara sewing in the little candle-lit parlour, almost simultaneously with a sudden downpour of rain came a knock at the front door. Jeremy, startled by this unwanted occurrence, went himself to answer the summons, and, opening the door, was confronted by a stout, youngish man dressed in black with elegant ruffles and a gold-headed cane.

"Your pardon, sir," said the new-comer, "but may I crave a moment's shelter during this shower? I am scarce equipped for the elements."

"Pray enter," said Jeremy hospitably.

"I am from London, and lodging at the 'White Hart' at Bullingford for the night," the stranger explained, shaking the rain-drops from his hat. "During a stroll before supper, I lost my way, and this storm has surprised me at your gate. I make a thousand apologies for deranging you."

"If you are wet the parlour fire will dry you. I beg you, sir, to follow me," said Jeremy. He led the way through the dark passage and, pausing with his hand on the door-knob, turned to the stranger and said with his grave courtesy:

"I think it right to warn you, sir, that I am afflicted with a certain personal disfigurement which not all persons can look upon with equanimity."

"Sir," replied the other, "my name is John Hattaway, surgeon at St. Thomas' Hospital in London, and I am used to regard with equanimity all forms of human affliction."

Mr. Hattaway was shown into the parlour and introduced in due form to Barbara. A chair was set for him near the fire. In the talk that followed he showed himself to be a man of parts and education. He was on his way, he said, to Oxford to perform an operation on the Warden of Merton College.

"What kind of operation?" asked Barbara.

His quick, keen eyes swept her like a searchlight.

"Madam," said he, not committing himself, "'tis but a slight one."

But when Barbara had left the room to mull some claret for her guest, Mr. Hattaway turned to Jeremy.

"'Tis a cataract," said he, "I am about to remove from the eye of the Warden of Merton by the new operation invented by my revered master, Mr. William Cheselden, my immediate predecessor at St. Thomas's. I did not tell your wife, for certain reasons; but I noticed that she is blinded by the same disease."

Jeremy rose from his chair.

"Do you mean that you will restore the Warden's sight?"

"I have every hope of doing so."

"But if his sight can be restored—then my wife's——"

"Can be restored also," said the surgeon complacently.

Jeremy sat down feeling faint and dizzy.

"Did you not know that cataract was curable?"

"I am scholar enough," answered Jeremy, "to have read that King John of Aragon was so cured by the Jew, Abiathar of Lerida, by means of a needle thrust through the eyeball——"

"Barbarous, my dear sir, barbarous!" cried the surgeon, raising a white, protesting hand. "One in a million may be so cured. There is even now a pestilential fellow of a quack, calling himself the Chevalier Taylor, who is prodding folks' eyes with a six-inch skewer. Have you never heard of him?"

"Alas, sir," said Jeremy, "I live so out of the world, and my daily converse is limited to my dear wife and the parson hard by, who is as recluse a scholar as I am myself."

"If you wish your wife to regain her sight," said Mr. Hattaway, "avoid this Chevalier Taylor like the very devil. But if you will intrust her to my care, Mr. Hattaway, surgeon of St. Thomas' Hospital, London, pupil of the great Cheselden——"

He waved his hand by way of completing the unfinished sentence.

"When?" asked Jeremy, greatly agitated.

"After her child is born."

"Shall I tell her?" Jeremy trembled.

"As you will. No—perhaps you had better wait a while."

Then Barbara entered, bearing a silver tray, with the mulled claret and glasses, proud of her blind surety of movement. Mr. Hattaway sprang to assist her and, unknown to her, took the opportunity of scrutinising her eyes. Then he nodded confidently at Jeremy.

VII

From that evening Jeremy's martyrdom began. Hitherto he had regarded the blindness of his wife as a special dispensation of Divine Providence. She had not seen him save on that first afternoon as a shadowy mass, and had formed no conception of his disfigurement beyond the vague impression conveyed to her by loving fingers touching his face. She had made her own mental picture of him, as she had said, and whatever it was, so far from repelling her, it pleased her mightily. Her ignorance indeed was bliss—for both of them. And now, thought poor Jeremy, knowledge would come with the restored vision, and, like our too-wise first parents, they would be driven out of Eden. Sometimes the devil entered his heart and prompted cowardly concealment. Why tell Barbara of Mr. Hattaway's proposal?

Why disturb a happiness already so perfect? All her other senses were eyes to her. She had grown almost unconscious of her affliction. She was happier loving him with blinded eyes than recoiling from him in horror with seeing ones. It was, in sooth, for her own dear happiness that she should remain in darkness. But then Jeremy remembered the only cry her brave soul had ever uttered, and after wrestling long in prayer he knew that the Evil One had spoken, and in the good, old-fashioned way he bade Satan get behind him. "*Retro me, Satanas*." The words are in his diary, printed in capital letters.

But one day, when she repeated her cry, his heart ached for her and he comforted her with the golden hope. She wept tears of joy and flung her arms around his neck and kissed him, and from that day forth filled the house with song and laughter and the mirth of unbounded happiness. But Jeremy, though he bespoke her tenderly and hopefully, felt that he had signed his death-warrant. Now and then, when her gay spirit danced through the glowing future, he was tempted to say: "When you see me as I am your love will turn to loathing and our heaven to hell." But he could not find it in his heart to dash her joy. And she never spoke of seeing him—only of seeing the child and the sun and the flowers and the buttons of his shirts, which she vowed must seem to be sewn on by a drunken cobbler.

VIII

The child was born, a boy, strong and lusty—to Jeremy the incarnation of miraculous wonder. That the thing was alive, with legs and arms and feet and hands, and could utter sounds, which it did with much vigour, made demands almost too great on his credulity.

"What is he like?" asked Barbara.

This was a poser for Jeremy. For the pink brat was like nothing on earth—save any other newborn infant.

"I think," he said hesitatingly, "I think he may be said to resemble Cupid. He has a mouth like Cupid's bow."

"And Cupid's wings?" she laughed. "Fie, Jeremy, I thought we had born to us a Christian child."

"But that he has a body," said Jeremy, "I should say he was a cherub. He has eyes of a celestial blue, and his nose——"

"Yes, yes, his nose?" came breathlessly from Barbara.

"I'm afraid, my dear, there is so little of it to judge by," said Jeremy.

"Before the summer's out I shall be able to judge for myself," said Barbara, and terror gripped the man's heart.

The days passed, and Barbara rose from her bed and again sang and laughed.

"See, I am strong enough to withstand any operation," she declared one day, holding out the babe at arm's length.

"Not yet," said Jeremy, "not yet. The child needs you."

The child was asleep. She felt with her foot for its cradle, and with marvellous certainty deposited him gently in the nest and covered him with the tiny coverlet. Then she turned to Jeremy.

"My husband, don't you wish me to have my sight restored?"

"How can you doubt it?" he cried. "I would have you undergo this operation were my life the fee."

She came close to him and put her hands about his maimed face. "Dear," she said, "do you think anything could change my love for you?"

It was the first hint that she had divined his fears; but he remained silent, every fibre of his being shrinking from the monstrous argument. For an answer, he kissed her hands as she withdrew them.

At last the time came for the great adventure. Letters passed between Jeremy and Mr. Hattaway of St. Thomas' Hospital, who engaged lodgings in Cork Street, so that they should be near his own residence in Bond Street hard by. A great travelling chariot and post-horses were hired from Bullingford, two great horsepistols, which Jeremy had never fired off in his life, were loaded and primed and put in the holsters, and one morning in early August Jeremy and Barbara and the nurse and the baby started on their perilous journey. They lay at Reading that night and arrived without misadventure at Cork Street on the following afternoon. Mr. Hattaway called in the evening with two lean and solemn young men, his apprentices—for even the great Mr. Hattaway was but a barber-surgeon practising a trade under the control of a City Guild—and made his preparations for the morrow.

In these days of anæsthetics and cocaine, sterilised instruments, trained nurses and scientific ventilation it is almost impossible to realise the conditions under which surgical operations were conducted in the first half of the eighteenth century. Yet they occasionally were successful, and patients sometimes did survive, and nobody complained, thinking, like Barbara Wendover, that all was for the best in this best of all possible worlds. For, as she lay in the close, darkened room the next day, after the operation was over, tended by a chattering beldame of a midwife, she took the burning pain in her bandaged eyes—after the dare-devil fashion of the time Mr. Hattaway had operated on both at once—as part of the cure, and thanked God she was born into so marvellous an epoch. Then Jeremy came and sat by her bed and held her hand, and she was very happy.

But Jeremy then, and in the slow, torturing days that followed, went about shrunken like a man doomed to worse than death. London increased his agony. At first a natural curiosity (for he had passed through the town but twice before, once as he set out for the grand tour with Doctor Tubbs, and once on his return thence) and a countryman's craving for air took him out into the busy streets. But he found the behaviour of the populace far different from that of the inhabitants of Bullingford, who passed him by respectfully, though with averted faces. Porters and lackeys openly jeered at him, ragged children summoned their congeners and followed hooting in his train; it was a cruel age, and elegant gentlemen in flowered silk coats and lace ruffles had no compunction in holding their cambric handkerchiefs before their eyes and vowing within his hearing that, stab their vitals, such a fellow should wear a mask or be put into the Royal Society's Museum; and in St. James's Street one fine lady, stepping out of her sedan-chair almost into his arms, fell back shrieking that she had seen a monster, and pretended to faint as the obsequious staymaker ran out of his shop to her assistance.

He ceased to go abroad in daylight and only crept about the streets at night, even then nervously avoiding the glare of a chance-met linkboy's torch. Desperate thoughts came to him during these gloomy rambles. Fear of God alone, as is evident from the diary, prevented him from taking his life. And the poor wretch prayed for he knew not what.

IX

One morning Mr. Hattaway, after his examination of the patient, entered the parlour where Jeremy was reading *Tillotson's Sermons* (there were fourteen volumes of them in the room's unlively bookcase) and closed the door behind him with an air of importance.

"Sir," said he, "I bring you good news."

Jeremy closed his book.

"She sees?"

"On removing the bandages just now," replied Mr. Hattaway, "I perceived to my great regret that with the left eye my skill has been unavailing. The failure is due, I believe, to an injury to the retina which I have been unable to discover." He paused and took snuff. "But I rejoice to inform you that sight is restored to the right eye. I admitted light into the room, and though the vision is diffused, which a lens will rectify, she saw me distinctly."

"Thank God she has the blessing of sight," said Jeremy reverently.

"Amen," said the surgeon. He took another pinch. "Also, perhaps, thank your humble servant for restoring it."

"I owe you an unpayable debt," replied Jeremy.

"She is crying out for the baby," said Mr. Hattaway. "If you will kindly send it in to her I can allow her a fleeting glimpse of it before I complete the rebandaging for the day."

Jeremy rang the bell and gave the order. "And I?" he inquired bravely.

The surgeon hesitated and scratched his plump cheeks.

"You know that my wife has never seen me."

"To-morrow, then," said Hattaway.

The nurse and child appeared at the doorway, and the surgeon followed them into Barbara's room.

When the surgeon had left the house Jeremy went to Barbara and found her crooning over the babe, which lay in her arms.

"I've seen him, dear, I've seen him!" she cried joyously. "He is the most wonderfully beautiful thing on the earth. His eyes are light blue, and mine are dark, so he must have yours. And his mouth is made for kisses, and his expression is that of a babe born in Paradise."

Jeremy bent over and looked at the boy, who sniggered at him in a most paradisiacal fashion, and they talked parentwise over his perfections.

"Before we go back to Bullingford you will let me take a coach, Jeremy, and drive about the streets and show him to the town? I will hold him up and cry: 'Ladies and gentlemen, look! 'Tis the tenth wonder of the world. You only have this one chance of seeing him.'"

She rattled on in the gayest of moods, making him laugh in spite of the terror. The failure of the operation in the left eye she put aside as of no account. One eye was a necessity, but two were a mere luxury.

"And it is the little rogue that will reap the benefit," she cried, cuddling the child. "For, when he is naughty mammy will turn the blind side of her face to him."

"And will you turn the blind side of your face to me?" asked Jeremy with a quiver of the lips.

She took his hand and pressed it against her cheek.

"You have no faults, my beloved husband, for me to be blind to," she said, wilfully or not misunderstanding him.

Such rapture had the sight of the child given her that she insisted on its lying with her that night, a truckle-bed being placed in the room for the child's nurse. When Jeremy took leave of her before going to his own room he bent over her and whispered:

"To-morrow."

Her sweet lips—pathetically sweet below the bandage— parted in a smile—and they never seemed sweeter to the anguished man—and she also whispered, "To-morrow!" and kissed him.

He went away, and as he closed the door, he felt that it was the gate of Paradise shut against him forever.

He did not sleep that night, but spent it as a brave man spends the night before his execution. For, after all, Jeremy Wendover was a gallant gentlemen.

In the morning he went into Barbara's room before breakfast, as his custom was, and found her still gay and bubbling over with the joy of life. And when he was leaving her she stretched out her hands and clasped his maimed face, as she had done once before, and said the same reassuring words. Nothing could shake her immense, her steadfast love. But Jeremy, entering the parlour and catching sight of himself in the Queen Anne mirror over the mantle-piece, shuddered to the inmost roots of his being. She had no conception of what she vowed.

He was scarce through breakfast when Mr. Hattaway entered, a full hour before his usual time.

"I am in a prodigious hurry," said he, "for I must go post-haste into Norfolk, to operate on my Lord Winteringham for the stone. I have not a moment to lose, so I pray you to accompany me to your wife's bedchamber."

The awful moment had come. Jeremy courteously opened doors for the surgeon to pass through, and followed with death in his heart. When they entered the room he noticed that Barbara had caused the nurse's truckle-bed to be removed and that she was lying, demure as a nun, in a newly made bed. The surgeon flung the black curtains from the window and let the summer light filter through the linen blinds.

"We will have a longer exposure this morning," said he, "and to-morrow a little longer still, and so on until we can face the daylight altogether. Now, madam, if you please."

He busied himself with the bandages. Jeremy, on the other

side of the bed, stood clasping Barbara's hand: stood stock-still, with thumping heart, holding his breath, setting his teeth, nerving himself for the sharp, instinctive gasp, the reflex recoil, that he knew would be the death sentence of their love. And at that supreme moment he cursed himself bitterly for a fool for not having told her of his terror, for not having sufficiently prepared her for the devastating revelation. But now it was too late.

The bandages were removed. The surgeon bent down and peered into the eyes. He started back in dismay. Before her right eye he rapidly waved his finger.

"Do you see that?"

"No," said Barbara.

"My God, madam!" cried he, with a stricken look on his plump face, "what in the devil's name have you been doing with yourself?"

Great drops of sweat stood on Jeremy's brow.

"What do you mean?" he asked.

"She can't see. The eye is injured. Yesterday, save for the crystalline lens which I extracted, it was as sound as mine or yours."

"I was afraid something had happened," said Barbara in a matter-of-fact tone. "Baby was restive in the night and pushed his little fist into my eye."

"Good heavens, madam!" exclaimed the angry surgeon, "you don't mean to say that you took a young baby to sleep with you in your condition?"

Barbara nodded, as if found out in a trifling peccadillo. "I suppose I'm blind for ever?" she asked casually.

He examined the eye again. There was a moment's dead silence. Jeremy, white-lipped and haggard, hung on the verdict.

Then Hattaway rose, extended his arms and let them drop help-lessly against his sides.

"Yes," said he. "The sight is gone."

Jeremy put his hands to his head, staggered, and, overcome by the reaction from the terror and the shock of the unlooked-for calamity, fell in a faint on the floor.

After he had recovered and the surgeon had gone, promising to send his apprentice the next day to dress the eyes, which, for fear of inflammation, still needed tending, Jeremy sat by his wife's bedside with an aching heart.

"'Tis the will of God," said he gloomily. "We must not rebel against His decrees."

"But, you dear, foolish husband," she cried, half laughing, "who wants to rebel against them? Not I, of a certainty. I am the happiest woman in the world."

"'Tis but to comfort me that you say it," said Jeremy.

"'Tis the truth. Listen." She sought for his hand and con-tinued with sweet seriousness: "I was selfish to want to regain my sight; but my soul hungered to see my babe. And now that I have seen him I care not. Just that one little peep into the heaven of his face was all I wanted. And 'twas the darling wretch himself who settled that I should not have more." After a little she said, "Come nearer to me," and she drew his ear to her lips and whispered:

"Although I have not regained my sight, on the other hand I have not lost a thing far dearer—the face that I love which I made up of your voice and the plash of water and the sunset and the summer air." She kissed him. "My poor husband, how you must have suffered!"

And then Jeremy knew the great, brave soul of that woman whom the Almighty had given him to wife, and, as he puts it in his diary, he did glorify God exceedingly.

So when Barbara was able to travel again Jeremy sent for the great, roomy chariot and the horse-pistols and the post-horses, and they went back to Bullingford, where they spent the remainder of their lives in unclouded felicity.

II

THE CONQUEROR

Miss Winifred Goode sat in her garden in the shade of a clipped yew, an unopened novel on her lap, and looked at the gabled front of the Tudor house that was hers and had been her family's for many generations. In that house, Duns Hall, in that room beneath the southernmost gable, she had been born. From that house, save for casual absences rarely exceeding a month in duration, she had never stirred. All the drama, such as it was, of her life had been played in that house, in that garden. Up and down the parapeted stone terrace walked the ghosts of all those who had been dear to her—her father, a vague but cherished memory; a brother and a sister who had died during her childhood; her mother, dead three years since, to whose invalid and somewhat selfish needs she had devoted all her full young womanhood. Another ghost walked there, too; but that was the ghost of the living—a young man who had kissed and ridden away, twenty years ago. He had kissed her over there, under the old wistaria arbour at the end of the terrace. What particular meaning he had put into the kiss, loverly, brotherly, cousinly, friendly—for they had played together all their young lives, and were distantly connected—she had never been able to determine. In spite of his joy at leaving the lethargic country town of Dunsfield for America, their parting had been sad and sentimental. The kiss, at any rate, had been, on his side, one of sincere affection—an affection proven afterwards by a correspondence of twenty years. To her the kiss had been—well, the one and only kiss of her life, and she had treasured it in a neat little sacred casket in her heart. Since that far-off day no man had ever showed an inclination to kiss her, which, in one way, was strange, as she had been pretty and gentle and laughter-loving, qualities attractive to youths in search of a mate. But in another way it was not strange, as mate-seeking youths are rare as angels in Dunsfield, beyond whose limits Miss Goode had seldom strayed. Her romance had been one kiss, the girlish dreams of one man. At first, when he had gone fortune-hunting in America, she had fancied herself broken-hearted; but Time had soon touched her with healing fingers. Of late, freed from the slavery of a querulous bedside, she had grown in love with her unruffled and delicately ordered existence, in which the only irregular things were her herbaceous borders, between which she walked like a prim school-mistress among a crowd of bright but unruly children. She had asked nothing more from life than what she had—her little duties in the parish, her little pleasures in the neighbourhood, her good health, her old house, her trim lawns, her old-fashioned garden, her black cocker spaniels. As it was at forty, she thought, so should it be till the day of her death.

But a month ago had come turmoil. Roger Orme announced his return. Fortune-making in America had tired him. He was coming home to settle down for good in Dunsfield, in the house of his fathers. This was Duns Lodge, whose forty acres marched with the two hundred acres of Duns Hall. The two places were known in the district as "The Lodge" and "The Hall." About a century since, a younger son of The Hall had married a daughter of The Lodge, whence the remote tie of consanguinity between Winifred Goode and Roger Orme. The Lodge had been let on lease for many years, but now the lease had fallen in and the tenants gone. Roger had arrived in England yesterday. A telegram had bidden her expect him that afternoon. She sat in the garden expecting him, and stared wistfully at the old grey house, a curious fear in her eyes.

Perhaps, if freakish chance had not brought Mrs. Donovan to Dunsfield on a visit to the Rector, a day or two after Roger's letter, fear—foolish, shameful, sickening fear—might not have had so dominant a place in her anticipation of his homecoming. Mrs. Donovan was a contemporary, a Dunsfield girl, who had married at nineteen and gone out with her husband to India. Winifred Goode remembered a gipsy beauty riotous in the bloom of youth. In the Rector's drawing-room she met a grey-haired, yellow-skinned, shrivelled caricature, and she looked in the woman's face as in a mirror of awful truth in which she herself was reflected. From that moment she had known no peace. Gone was her placid acceptance of the footprints of the years, gone her old-maidish pride in dainty, old-maidish dress. She had mixed little with the modern world, and held to old-fashioned prejudices which prescribed the outward demeanour appropriate to each decade. One of her earliest memories was a homely saying of her father's—which had puzzled her childish mind considerably—as to the absurdity of sheep being dressed lamb fashion. Later she understood and cordially agreed with the dictum. The Countess of Ingleswood, the personage of those latitudes, at the age of fifty showed the fluffy golden hair and peach-bloom cheeks and supple figure of twenty; she wore bright colours and dashing hats, and danced and flirted and kept a tame-cattery of adoring young men. Winifred visited with Lady Ingleswood because she believed that, in these democratic days, it was the duty of county families to outmatch the proletariat in solidarity; but, with every protest of her gentlewoman's soul, she disapproved of Lady Ingleswood. Yet now, to her appalling dismay, she saw that, with the aid of paint, powder, and peroxide, Lady Ingleswood had managed to keep young. For thirty years, to Winifred's certain knowledge, she had not altered. The blasting hand that had swept over Madge Donovan's face had passed her by.

Winifred envied the woman's power of attraction. She read, with a curious interest, hitherto disregarded advertisements. They were so alluring, they seemed so convincing. Such a cosmetic used by queens of song and beauty restored the roses of girlhood; under such a treatment, wrinkles disappeared within a week—there were the photographs to prove it. All over London bubbled fountains of youth, at a mere guinea or so a dip. She sent for a little battery of washes and powders, and, when it arrived, she locked herself in her bedroom. But the sight of the first unaccustomed—and unskilfully applied—dab of rouge on her cheek terrified her. She realised what she was doing. No! Ten thousand times no! Her old-maidishness, her puritanism revolted. She flew to her hand-basin and vigorously washed the offending bloom away with soap and water. She would appear before the man she loved just as she was—if need be, in the withered truth of a Madge Donovan.... And, after all, had her beauty faded so utterly? Her glass said "No." But her glass mocked her, for how could she conjure up the young face of twenty which Roger Orme carried in his mind, and compare it with the present image?

She sat in the garden, this blazing July afternoon, waiting for him, her heart beating with the love of years ago, and the shrinking fear in her eyes. Presently she heard the sound of wheels, and she saw the open fly of "The Red Lion"—Dunsfield's chief hotel—crawling up the drive, and in it was a man wearing a straw hat. She fluttered a timid handkerchief, but the man, not looking in her direction, did not respond. She crossed the lawn to the terrace, feeling hurt, and entered the drawing-room by the open French window and stood there, her back to the light. Soon he was announced. She went forward to meet him.

"My dear Roger, welcome home."

He laughed and shook her hand in a hearty grip.

"It's you, Winifred. How good! Are you glad to see me back?"

"Very glad."

"And I."

"Do you find things changed?"

"Nothing," he declared with a smile; "the house is just the same." He ran his fingers over the corner of a Louis XVI table near which he was standing. "I remember this table, in this exact spot, twenty years ago."

"And you have scarcely altered. I should have known you anywhere."

"I should just hope so," said he.

She realised, with a queer little pang, that time had improved the appearance of the man of forty-five. He was tall, strong, erect; few accusing lines marked his clean-shaven, florid, clear-cut face; in his curly brown hair she could not detect a touch of grey. He had a new air of mastery and success which expressed itself in the corners of his firm lips and the steady, humorous gleam in his eyes.

"You must be tired after your hot train journey," she said.

He laughed again. "Tired? After a couple of hours? Now, if it had been a couple of days, as we are accustomed to on the other side—— But go on talking, just to let me keep on hearing your voice. It's yours—I could have recognised it over a long-distance telephone—and it's English. You've no idea how delicious it is. And the smell of the room"—he drew in a deep breath—"is you and the English country. I tell you, it's good to be back!"

She flushed, his pleasure was so sincere, and she smiled.

"But why should we stand? Let me take your hat and stick."

"Why shouldn't we sit in the garden—after my hot and tiring journey?" They both laughed. "Is the old wistaria still there, at the end of the terrace?"

She turned her face away. "Yes, still there. Do you remember it?" she asked in a low voice.

"Do you think I could forget it? I remember every turn of the house."

"Let us go outside, then."

She led the way, and he followed, to the trellis arbour, a few steps from the drawing-room door. The long lilac blooms had gone with the spring, but the luxuriant summer leafage cast a grateful shade. Roger Orme sat in a wicker chair and fanned himself with his straw hat.

"Delightful!" he said. "And I smell stocks! It does carry me back. I wonder if I have been away at all."

"I'm afraid you have," said Winifred—"for twenty years."

"Well, I'm not going away again. I've had my share of work. And what's the good of work just to make money? I've made enough. I sold out before I left."

"But in your letters you always said you liked America."

"So I did. It's the only country in the world for the young and eager. If I had been born there, I should have no use for Dunsfield. But a man born and bred among old, sleepy things has the nostalgia of old, sleepy things in his blood. Now tell me about the sleepy old things. I want to hear."

"I think I have written to you about everything that ever happened in Dunsfield," she said.

But still there were gaps to be bridged in the tale of births and marriages and deaths, the main chronicles of the neighbourhood. He had a surprising memory, and plucked obscure creatures from the past whom even Winifred had forgotten.

"It's almost miraculous how you remember."

"It's a faculty I've had to cultivate," said he.

They talked about his immediate plans. He was going to put The Lodge into thorough repair, bring everything up-to-date, lay in electric light and a central heating installation, fix bathrooms wherever bathrooms would go, and find a place somewhere for a billiard-room. His surveyor had already made his report, and was to meet him at the house the following morning. As for decorations, curtaining, carpeting, and such-like æsthetic aspects, he was counting on Winifred's assistance. He thought that blues and browns would harmonise with the oak-panelling in the dining-room. Until the house was ready, his headquarters would be "The Red Lion."

"You see, I'm going to begin right now," said he.

She admired his vitality, his certainty of accomplishment. The Hall was still lit by lamps and candles; and although, on her return from a visit, she had often deplored the absence of electric light, she had shrunk from the strain and worry of an innovation. And here was Roger turning the whole house inside out more cheerfully than she would turn out a drawer.

"You'll help me, won't you?" he asked. "I want a home with a touch of the woman in it; I've lived so long in masculine stiffness."

"You know that I should love to do anything I could, Roger," she replied happily.

He remarked again that it was good to be back. No more letters—they were unsatisfactory, after all. He hoped she had not resented his business man's habit of typewriting. This was in the year of grace eighteen hundred and ninety-two, and, save for Roger's letters, typewritten documents came as seldom as judgment summonses to Duns Hall.

"We go ahead in America," said he.

"'The old order changeth, yielding place to new.' I accept it," she said with a smile.

"What I've longed for in Dunsfield," he said, "is the old order that doesn't change. I don't believe anything has changed."

She plucked up her courage. Now she would challenge him—get it over at once. She would watch his lips as he answered.

"I'm afraid I must have changed, Roger."

"In what way?"

"I am no longer twenty."

"Your voice is just the same."

Shocked, she put up her delicate hands. "Don't—it hurts!"

"What?"

"You needn't have put it that way—you might have told a polite lie."

He rose, turned aside, holding the back of the wicker chair.

"I've got something to tell you," he said abruptly. "You would have to find out soon, so you may as well know now. But don't be alarmed or concerned. I can't see your face."

"What do you mean?"

"I've been stone blind for fifteen years."

"Blind?"

She sat for some moments paralysed. It was inconceivable. This man was so strong, so alive, so masterful, with the bright face and keen, humorous eyes—and blind! A trivial undercurrent of thought ran subconsciously beneath her horror. She had wondered why he had insisted on sounds and scents, why he had kept his stick in his hand, why he had touched things—tables, window jambs, chairs—now she knew. Roger went on talking, and she heard him in a dream. He had not informed her when he was stricken, because he had wished to spare her unnecessary anxiety. Also, he was proud, perhaps hard, and resented sympathy. He had made up his mind to win through in spite of his affliction. For some years it had been the absorbing passion of his life. He had won through like many another, and, as the irreparable detachment of the retina had not disfigured his eyes, it was his joy to go through the world like a seeing man, hiding his blindness from the casual observer. By dictated letter he could never have made her understand how trifling a matter it was.

"And I've deceived even you!" he laughed.

Tears had been rolling down her cheeks. At his laugh she gave way. An answering choke, hysterical, filled her throat, and she burst into a fit of sobbing. He laid his hand tenderly on her head.

"My dear, don't. I am the happiest man alive. And, as for eyes, I'm rich enough to buy a hundred pairs. I'm a perfect Argus!"

But Winifred Goode wept uncontrollably. There was deep pity for him in her heart, but—never to be revealed to mortal —there was also horrible, terrifying joy. She gripped her hands and sobbed frantically to keep herself from laughter. A woman's sense of humour is often cruel, only to be awakened by tragic incongruities. She had passed through her month's agony and shame for a blind man.

At last she mastered herself. "Forgive me, dear Roger. It was a dreadful shock. Blindness has always been to me too awful for thought—like being buried alive."

"Not a bit of it," he said cheerily. "I've run a successful business in the dark—real estate—buying and selling and developing land, you know—a thing which requires a man to keep a sharp look-out, and which he couldn't do if he were buried alive. It's a confounded nuisance, I admit, but so is gout. Not half as irritating as the position of a man I once knew who had both hands cut off."

She shivered. "That's horrible."

"It is," said he, "but blindness isn't."

The maid appeared with the tea-tray, which she put on a

rustic table. It was then that Winifred noticed the little proud awkwardness of the blind man. There was pathos in his insistent disregard of his affliction. The imperfectly cut lower half of a watercress sandwich fell on his coat and stayed there. She longed to pick it off, but did not dare, for fear of hurting him. He began to talk again of the house—the scheme of decoration.

"Oh, it all seems so sad!" she cried.

"What?"

"You'll not be able to see the beautiful things."

"Good Heavens," he retorted, "do you think I am quite devoid of imagination? And do you suppose no one will enter the house but myself?"

"I never thought of that," she admitted.

"As for the interior, I've got a plan in my head, and could walk about it now blindfold, only that's unnecessary; and when it's all fixed up, I'll have a ground model made of every room, showing every piece of furniture, so that, when I get in, I'll know the size, shape, colour, quality of every blessed thing in the house. You see if I don't."

"These gifts are a merciful dispensation of Providence."

"Maybe," said he drily. "Only they were about the size of bacteria when I started, and it took me years of incessant toil to develop them."

He asked to be shown around the garden. She took him up the gravelled walks beside her gay borders and her roses, telling him the names and varieties of the flowers. Once he stopped and frowned.

"I've lost my bearings. We ought to be passing under the shade of the old walnut tree."

"You are quite right," she said, marvelling at his accuracy. "It stood a few steps back, but it was blown clean down three years ago. It had been dead for a long time."

He chuckled as he strolled on. "There's nothing makes me so mad as to be mistaken."

Some time later, on their return to the terrace, he held out his hand.

"But you'll stay for dinner, Roger," she exclaimed. "I can't bear to think of you spending your first evening at home in that awful 'Red Lion.'"

"That's very dear of you, Winnie," he said, evidently touched by the softness in her voice. "I'll dine with pleasure, but I must get off some letters first. I'll come back. You've no objection to my bringing my man with me?"

"Why, of course not." She laid her hand lightly on his arm. "Oh, Roger, dear, I wish I could tell you how sorry I am, how my heart aches for you!"

"Don't worry," he said—"don't worry a little bit, and, if you really want to help me, never let me feel that you notice I'm blind. Forget it, as I do."

"I'll try," she said.

"That's right." He held her hand for a second or two, kissed it, and dropped it, abruptly. "God bless you!" said he. "It's good to be with you again."

When he was gone, Winifred Goode returned to her seat by the clipped yew and cried a little, after the manner of women. And, after the manner of women, she dreamed dreams oblivious of the flight of time till her maid came out and hurried her indoors.

She dressed with elaborate care, in her best and costliest, and wore more jewels than she would have done had her guest been of normal sight, feeling oddly shaken by the thought of his intense imaginative vision. In trying to fasten the diamond clasp of a velvet band round her neck, her fingers trembled so much that the maid came to her assistance. Her mind was in a whirl. Roger had left her a headstrong, dissatisfied boy. He had returned, the romantic figure of a conqueror, all the more romantic and conquering by reason of his triumph over the powers of darkness. In his deep affection she knew her place was secure. The few hours she had passed with him had shown her that he was a man trained in the significance not only of words, but also of his attitude towards individual men and women. He would not have said "God bless you!" unless he meant it. She appreciated to the full his masculine strength; she took to her heart his masculine tenderness; she had a woman's pity for his affliction; she felt unregenerate exultancy at the undetected crime of lost beauty, and yet she feared him on account of the vanished sense. She loved him with a passionate recrudescence of girlish sentiment; but the very thing that might have, that ought to have, that she felt it indecent not to have, inflamed all her woman's soul and thrown her reckless into his arms, raised between them an impalpable barrier against which she dreaded lest she might be dashed and bruised.

At dinner this feeling was intensified. Roger made little or no allusion to his blindness; he talked with the ease of the cultivated man of the world. He had humour, gaiety, charm. As a mere companion, she had rarely met, during her long seclusion, a man so instinctive in sympathy, so quick in diverting talk into a channel of interest. In a few flashing yet subtle questions, he learned what she wore. The diamond clasp to the black velvet band he recognized as having been her mother's. He complimented her delicately on her appearance, as though he saw her clearly, in the adorable twilight beauty that was really hers. There were moments when it seemed impossible that he should be blind. But behind his chair, silent, impassive, arresting, freezing, hovered his Chinese body-servant, capped, pigtailed, loosely clad in white, a creature as unreal in Dunsfield as gnome or merman, who, with the unobtrusiveness of a shadow from another world, served, in the mechanics of the meal, as an accepted, disregarded, and unnoticed pair of eyes for his master. The noble Tudor dining-room, with its great carved oak chimney-piece, its stately gilt-framed portraits, its Jacobean sideboards and presses, all in the gloom of the spent illumination of the candles on the daintily-set table, familiar to her from her earliest childhood, part of her conception of the cosmos, part of her very self, seemed metamorphosed into the unreal, the phantasmagoric, by the presence of this white-clad, exotic figure—not a man, but an eerie embodiment of the sense of sight.

Her reason told her that the Chinese servant was but an ordinary serving-man, performing minutely specified duties for a generous wage. But the duties were performed magically, like conjurer's tricks. It was practically impossible to say who cut up Roger's meat, who helped him to salt or to vegetables, who guided his hand unerringly to the wine glass. So abnormally exquisite was the co-ordination between the two, that Roger seemed to have the man under mesmeric control. The idea bordered on the monstrous. Winifred shivered through the dinner, in spite of Roger's bright talk, and gratefully welcomed the change of the drawing-room, whither the white-vestured automaton did not follow.

"Will you do me a favour, Winnie?" he asked during the evening. "Meet me at The Lodge tomorrow at eleven, and help me interview these building people. Then you can have a finger in the pie from the very start."

She said somewhat tremulously: "Why do you want me to have a finger in the pie?"

"Good Heavens," he cried, "aren't you the only human creature in this country I care a straw about?"

"Is that true, Roger?"

"Sure," said he. After a little span of silence he laughed.

"People on this side don't say 'sure.' That's sheer American."

"I like it," said Winifred.

When he parted from her, he again kissed her hand and again said: "God bless you!" She accompanied him to the hall, where the Chinaman, ghostly in the dimness, was awaiting him with hat and coat. Suddenly she felt that she abhorred the Chinaman.

That night she slept but little, striving to analyse her feelings. Of one fact only did the dawn bring certainty—that, for all her love of him, for all his charm, for all his tenderness towards her, during dinner she had feared him horribly.

She saw him the next morning in a new and yet oddly familiar phase. He was attended by his secretary, a pallid man with a pencil, note-book, and documents, forever at his elbow, ghostly, automatic, during their wanderings with the surveyor through the bare and desolate old house.

She saw the master of men at work, accurate in every detail of a comprehensive scheme, abrupt, imperious, denying difficulties with harsh impatience. He leaned over his secretary and pointed to portions of the report just as though he could read them, and ordered their modification.

"Mr. Withers," he said once to the surveyor, who was raising objections, "I always get what I want because I make dead sure that what I want is attainable. I'm not an idealist. If I say a thing is to be done, it has got to be done, and it's up to you or to someone else to do it."

They went through the house from furnace to garret, the pallid secretary ever at Roger's elbow, ever rendering him imperceptible services, ever identifying himself with the sightless man, mysteriously following his thoughts, coordinating his individuality with that of his master. He was less a man than a trained faculty, like the Chinese servant. And again Winifred shivered and felt afraid.

More and more during the weeks that followed, did she realize the iron will and irresistible force of the man she loved. He seemed to lay a relentless grip on all those with whom he came in contact and compel them to the expression of himself. Only towards her was he gentle and considerate. Many times she accompanied him to London to the great shops, the self-effacing secretary shadow-like at his elbow, and discussed with him colours and materials, and he listened to her with affectionate deference. She often noticed that the secretary translated into other terms her description of things. This irritated her, and once she suggested leaving the secretary behind. Surely, she urged, she could do all that was necessary. He shook his head.

"No, my dear," he said very kindly. "Jukes sees for me. I shouldn't like you to see for me in the way Jukes does."

She was the only person from whom he would take advice or suggestion, and she rendered him great service in the tasteful equipment of the house and in the engagement of a staff of servants. So free a hand did he allow her in certain directions, so obviously and deliberately did he withdraw from her sphere of operations, that she was puzzled. It was not until later, when she knew him better, that the picture vaguely occurred to her of him caressing her tenderly with one hand, and holding the rest of the world by the throat with the other.

On the day when he took up his residence in the new home, they walked together through the rooms. In high spirits, boyishly elated, he gave her an exhibition of his marvellous gifts of memory, minutely describing each bit of furniture and its position in every room, the colour scheme, the texture of curtains, the pictures on the walls, the knick-knacks on mantle pieces and tables. And when he had done, he put his arm around her shoulders.

"But for you, Winnie," said he, "this would be the dreariest possible kind of place; but the spirit of you pervades it and makes it a fragrant paradise."

The words and tone were lover-like, and so was his clasp. She felt very near him, very happy, and her heart throbbed quickly. She was ready to give her life to him.

"You are making me a proud woman," she murmured.

He patted her shoulder and laughed as he released her.

"I only say what's true, my dear," he replied, and then abruptly skipped from sentiment to practical talk.

Winifred had a touch of dismay and disappointment. Tears started, which she wiped away furtively. She had made up her mind to accept him, in spite of Wang Fu and Mr. Jukes, if he should make her a proposal of marriage. She had been certain that the moment had come. But he made no proposal.

She waited. She waited a long time. In the meanwhile, she continued to be Roger's intimate friend and eagerly-sought companion. One day his highly-paid and efficient housekeeper came to consult her. The woman desired to give notice. Her place was too difficult. She could scarcely believe the master was blind. He saw too much, he demanded too much. She could say nothing explicit, save that she was frightened. She wept, after the nature of upset housekeepers. Winifred soothed her and advised her not to throw up so lucrative a post, and, as soon as she had an opportunity, she spoke to Roger. He laughed his usual careless laugh.

"They all begin that way with me, but after a while they're broken in. You did quite right to tell Mrs. Strode to stay."

And after a few months Winifred saw a change in Mrs. Strode, and not only in Mrs. Strode, but in all the servants whom she had engaged. They worked the household like parts of a flawless machine. They grew to be imperceptible, shadowy, automatic, like Wang Fu and Mr. Jukes.

*****

The months passed and melted into years. Roger Orme became a great personage in the neighbourhood. He interested himself in local affairs, served on the urban district council and on boards innumerable. They made him Mayor of Dunsfield. He subscribed largely to charities and entertained on a sumptuous scale. He ruled the little world, setting a ruthless heel on proud necks and making the humble his instruments. Mr. Jukes died, and other secretaries came, and those who were not instantly dismissed grew to be like Mr. Jukes. In the course of time Roger entered Parliament as member for the division. He became a force in politics, in public affairs. In the appointment of Royal Commissions, committees of inquiry, his name was the first to occur to ministers, and he was invariably respected, dreaded, and hated by his colleagues.

"Why do you work so hard, Roger?" Winifred would ask.

He would say, with one of his laughs: "Because there's a dynamo in me that I can't stop."

And all these years Miss Winifred Goode stayed at Duns Hall, leading her secluded, lavender-scented life when Roger was in London, and playing hostess for him, with diffident graciousness, when he entertained at The Lodge. His attitude towards her never varied, his need of her never lessened.

He never asked her to be his wife. At first she wondered, pined a little, and then, like a brave, proud woman, put the matter behind her. But she knew that she counted for much in his strange existence, and the knowledge comforted her. And as the years went on, and all the lingering shreds of youth left her, and she grew gracefully into the old lady, she came to regard her association with him as a spiritual marriage.

Then, after twenty years, the dynamo wore out the fragile tenement of flesh. Roger Orme, at sixty-five, broke down and lay on his death-bed. One day he sent for Miss Winifred Goode.

She entered the sick-room, a woman of sixty, white-haired, wrinkled, with only the beauty of a serene step across the threshold of old age. He bade the nurse leave them alone, and put out his hand and held hers as she sat beside the bed.

"What kind of a day is it, Winnie?"

"As if you didn't know! You've been told, I'm sure, twenty times."

"What does it matter what other people say? I want to get at the day through you."

"It's bright and sunny—a perfect day of early summer."

"What things are out?"

"The may and the laburnum and the lilac——"

"And the wistaria?"

"Yes, the wistaria."

"It's forty years ago, dear, and your voice is just the same. And to me you have always been the same. I can see you as you sit there, with your dear, sensitive face, the creamy cheek, in which the blood comes and goes—oh, Heavens, so different from the blowsy, hard-featured girls nowadays, who could not blush if—well—well——I know 'em, although I'm blind—I'm Argus, you know, dear. Yes, I can see you, with your soft, brown eyes and pale brown hair waved over your pure brow. There is a fascinating little kink on the left-hand side. Let me feel it."

She drew her head away, frightened. Then suddenly she remembered, with a pang of thankfulness, that the queer little kink had defied the years, though the pale brown hair was white. She guided his hand and he felt the kink, and he laughed in his old, exultant way.

"Don't you think I'm a miracle, Winnie?"

"You're the most wonderful man living," she said.

"I shan't be living long. No, my dear, don't talk platitudes. I know. I'm busted. And I'm glad I'm going before I begin to dodder. A seeing dodderer is bad enough, but a blind dodderer's only fit for the grave. I've lived my life. I've proved to this stupendous clot of ignorance that is humanity that a blind man can guide them wherever he likes. You know I refused a knighthood. Any tradesman can buy a knighthood—the only knighthoods that count are those that are given to artists and writers and men of science—and, if I could live, I'd raise hell over the matter, and make a differentiation in the titles of honour between the great man and the rascally cheesemonger——"

"My dear," said Miss Winifred Goode, "don't get so excited."

"I'm only saying, Winnie, that I refused a knighthood. But— what I haven't told you, what I'm supposed to keep a dead secret—if I could live a few weeks longer, and I shan't, I should be a Privy Councillor—a thing worth being. I've had the official intimation—a thing that can't be bought. Heavens, if I were a younger man, and there were the life in me, I should be the Prime Minister of this country—the first great blind ruler that ever was in the world. Think of it! But I don't want anything now. I'm done. I'm glad. The whole caboodle is but leather and prunella. There is only one thing in the world that is of any importance."

"What is that, dear?" she asked quite innocently, accustomed to, but never familiar with, his vehement paradox.

"Love," said he.

He gripped her hand hard. There passed a few seconds of tense silence.

"Winnie, dear," he said at last, "will you kiss me?"

She bent forward, and he put his arm around her neck and

drew her to him. They kissed each other on the lips.

"It's forty years since I kissed you, dear—that day under the wistaria. And, now I'm dying, I can tell you. I've loved you all the time, Winnie. I'm a tough nut, as you know, and whatever I do I do intensely. I've loved you intensely, furiously."

She turned her head away, unable to bear the living look in the sightless eyes.

"Why did you never tell me?" she asked in a low voice.

"Would you have married me?"

"You know I would, Roger."

"At first I vowed I would say nothing," he said, after a pause, "until I had a fit home to offer you. Then the blindness came, and I vowed I wouldn't speak until I had conquered the helplessness of my affliction. Do you understand?"

"Yes, but when you came home a conqueror——"

"I loved you too much to marry you. You were far too dear and precious to come into the intimacy of my life. Haven't you seen what happened to all those who did?" He raised his old knotted hands, clenched tightly. "I squeezed them dry. I couldn't help it. My blindness made me a coward. It has been hell. The darkness never ceased to frighten me. I lied when I said it didn't matter. I stretched out my hands like tentacles and gripped everyone within reach in a kind of madness of self-preservation. I made them give up their souls and senses to me. It was some ghastly hypnotic power I seemed to have. When I got them, they lost volition, individuality. They were about as much living creatures to me as my arm or my foot. Don't you see?"

The white-haired woman looked at the old face working passionately, and she felt once more the deadly fear of him.

"But with me it would have been different," she faltered.

"You say you loved me."

"That's the devil of it, my sweet, beautiful Winnie—it wouldn't have been different. I should have squeezed you, too, reduced you to the helpless thing that did my bidding, sucked your life's blood from you. I couldn't have resisted. So I kept you away. Have I ever asked you to use your eyes for me?"

Her memory travelled down the years, and she was amazed. She remembered Mr. Jukes at the great shops and many similar incidents that had puzzled her.

"No," she said.

There was a short silence. The muscles of his face relaxed, and the old, sweet smile came over it. He reached for her hand and caressed it tenderly.

"By putting you out of my life, I kept you, dear. I kept you as the one beautiful human thing I had. Every hour of happiness I have had for the last twenty years has come through you."

She said tearfully: "You have been very good to me, Roger."

"It's a queer mix-up, isn't it?" he said, after a pause. "Most people would say that I've ruined your life. If it hadn't been for me, you might have married."

"No, dear," she replied. "I've had a very full and happy life."

The nurse came into the room to signify the end of the visit, and found them hand in hand like lovers. He laughed.

"Nurse," said he, "you see a dying but a jolly happy old man!"

Two days afterwards Roger Orme died. On the afternoon of the funeral, Miss Winifred Goode sat in the old garden in the shade of the clipped yew, and looked at the house in which she had been born, and in which she had passed her sixty years of life, and at the old wistaria beneath which he had kissed her forty years ago. She smiled and murmured aloud:

"No, I would not have had a single thing different."

III

A LOVER'S DILEMMA

"How are you feeling now?"

Words could not express the music of these six liquid syllables that fell through the stillness and the blackness on my ears.

"Not very bright, I'm afraid, nurse," said I.

Think of something to do with streams and moonlight, and you may have an idea of the mellow ripple of the laugh I heard.

"I'm not the nurse. Can't you tell the difference? I'm Miss Deane—Dr. Deane's daughter."

"Deane?" I echoed.

"Don't you know where you are?"

"Everything is still confused," said I.

I had an idea that they had carried me somewhere by train and put me into a bed, and that soft-fingered people had tended my eyes; but where I was I neither knew nor cared. Torture and blindness had been quite enough to occupy my mind.

"You are at Dr. Deane's house," said the voice, "and Dr. Deane is the twin brother of Mr. Deane, the great oculist of Grandchester, who was summoned to Shepton-Marling when you met with your accident. Perhaps you know you had a gun accident?"

"I suppose it was only that after all," said I, "but it felt like the disruption of the solar system."

"Are you still in great pain?" my unseen hostess asked sympathetically.

"Not since you have been in the room. I mean," I added, chilled by a span of silence, "I mean—I am just stating what happens to be a fact."

"Oh!" she said shortly. "Well, my uncle found that you couldn't be properly treated at your friend's little place at Shepton-Marling, so he brought you to Grandchester—and here you are."

"But I don't understand," said I, "why I should be a guest in your house."

"You are not a guest," she laughed. "You are here on the most sordid and commercial footing. Your friend—I forget his name ____"

"Mobray," said I.

"Mr. Mobray settled it with my uncle. You see the house is large and father's practice small, as we keep a nursing home for my uncle's patients. Of course we have trained nurses."

"Are you one?" I asked.

"Not exactly. I do the housekeeping. But I can settle those uncomfortable pillows."

I felt her dexterous cool hands about my head and neck. For a moment or two my eyes ceased to ache, and I wished I could see her. In tendering my thanks, I expressed the wish. She laughed her delicious laugh.

"If you could see you wouldn't be here, and therefore you couldn't see me anyhow."

"Shall I ever see you?" I asked dismally.

"Why, of course! Don't you know that Henry Deane is one of

the greatest oculists in England?"

We discussed my case and the miraculous skill of Henry Deane. Presently she left me, promising to return. The tones of her voice seemed to linger, as perfume would, in the darkness.

That was the beginning of it. It was love, not at first sight, but at first sound. Pain and anxiety stood like abashed goblins at the back of my mind. Valerie Deane's voice danced in front like a triumphant fairy. When she came and talked sick-room platitudes I had sooner listened to her than to the music of the spheres. At that early stage what she said mattered so little. I would have given rapturous heed to her reading of logarithmic tables. I asked her silly questions merely to elicit the witchery of her voice. When Melba sings, do you take count of the idiot words? You close eyes and intellect and just let the divine notes melt into your soul. And when you are lying on your back, blind and helpless, as I was, your soul is a very sponge for anything beautiful that can reach it. After a while she gave me glimpses of herself, sweet and womanly; and we drifted from commonplace into deeper things. She was the perfect companion. We discussed all topics, from chiffons to Schopenhauer. Like most women, she execrated Schopenhauer. She must have devoted much of her time to me; yet I ungratefully complained of the long intervals between her visits. But oh! those interminable idle hours of darkness, in which all the thoughts that had ever been thought were rethought over and over again until the mind became a worn-out rag-bag! Only those who have been through the valley of this shadow can know its desolation. Only they can understand the magic of the unbeheld Valerie Deane.

"What is the meaning of this?" she asked one morning. "Nurse says you are fretful and fractious."

"She insisted on soaping the soles of my feet and tickling me into torments, which made me fractious, and I'm dying to see your face, which makes me fretful."

"Since when have you been dying?" she asked.

"From the first moment I heard your voice saying, 'How are you feeling now?' It's irritating to have a friend and not in the least know what she is like. Besides," I added, "your voice is so beautiful that your face must be the same."

She laughed.

"Your face is like your laugh," I declared.

"If my face were my fortune I should come off badly," she said in a light tone. I think she was leaning over the foot-rail, and I longed for her nearer presence.

"Nurse has tied this bandage a little too tightly," I said mendaciously.

I heard her move, and in a moment her fingers were busy about my eyes. I put up my hand and touched them. She patted my hand away.

"Please don't be foolish," she remarked. "When you recover your sight and find what an exceedingly plain girl I am, you'll go away like the others, and never want to see me again."

"What others?" I exclaimed.

"Do you suppose you're the only patient I have had to manage?"

I loathed "the others" with a horrible detestation; but I said, after reflection:

"Tell me about yourself. I know you are called Valerie from Dr. Deane. How old are you?"

She pinned the bandage in front of my forehead.

"Oh, I'm young enough," she answered with a laugh. "Three-and-twenty. And I'm five-foot-four, and I haven't a bad figure. But I haven't any good looks at all, at all."

"Tell me," said I impatiently, "exactly how you do look. I must know."

"I have a sallow complexion. Not very good skin. And a low forehead."

"An excellent thing," said I.

"But my eyebrows and hair run in straight parallel lines, so it isn't," she retorted. "It is very ugly. I have thin black hair."

"Let me feel."

"Certainly not. And my eyes are a sort of watery china blue and much too small. And my nose isn't a bad nose altogether, but it's fleshy. One of those nondescript, aristocratic noses that always looks as if it has got a cold. My mouth is large—I am looking at myself in the glass—my teeth are white. Yes, they are nice and white. But they are large and protrude—you know the French caricature of an Englishwoman's teeth. Really, now I consider the question, I am the image of the English *mees* in a French comic paper."

"I don't believe it," I declared.

"It is true. I know I have a pretty voice—but that is all. It deceives blind people. They think I must be pretty too, and when they see me—*bon soir, la compagnie*! And I've such a thin, miserable face, coming to the chin in a point, like a kite. There! Have you a clear idea of me now?"

"No," said I, "for I believe you are wilfully misrepresenting yourself. Besides, beauty does not depend upon features regular in themselves, but the way those features are put together."

"Oh, mine are arranged in an amiable sort of way. I don't look cross."

"You must look sweetness itself," said I.

She sighed and said meditatively:

"It is a great misfortune for a girl to be so desperately plain. The consciousness of it comes upon her like a cold shower-bath when she is out with other girls. Now there is my cousin——"

"Which cousin?"

"My Uncle Henry's daughter. Shall I tell you about her?"

"I am not in the least interested in your cousin," I replied.

She laughed, and the entrance of the nurse put an end to the conversation.

Now I must make a confession. I was grievously disappointed. Her detailed description of herself as a sallow, ill-featured young woman awoke me with a shock from my dreams of a radiant goddess. It arrested my infatuation in mid-course. My dismay was painful. I began to pity her for being so unattractive. For the next day or two even her beautiful voice failed in its seduction.

But soon a face began to dawn before me, elusive at first, and then gradually gaining in definition. At last the picture flashed upon my mental vision with sudden vividness, and it has never left me to this day. Its steadfastness convinced me of its accuracy. It was so real that I could see its expression vary, as she spoke, according to her mood. The plainness, almost ugliness, of the face repelled me. I thought ruefully of having dreamed of kisses from the lips that barely closed in front of the great white teeth. Yet, after a while, its higher qualities exercised a peculiar attraction. A brave, tender spirit shone through. An intellectual alertness redeemed the heavy features—the low ugly brow, the coarse nose, the large mouth; and as I lay thinking and picturing there was revealed in an illuminating flash the secret of the harmony between face and voice. Thenceforward Valerie Deane was invested with a beauty all her own. I loved the dear plain face as I loved the beautiful voice, and the touch of her fingers, and the tender, laughing womanliness, and all that went with the concept of Valerie Deane.

Had I possessed the daring of Young Lochinvar, I should, on several occasions, have declared my passion. But by temperament I am a diffident procrastinator. I habitually lose golden moments as some people habitually lose umbrellas. Alas! There is no Lost Property Office for golden moments!

Still I vow, although nothing definite was said, that when the unanticipated end drew near, our intercourse was arrant love-making.

All pain had gone from my eyes. I was up and dressed and permitted to grope my way about the blackness. To-morrow I was to have my first brief glimpse of things for three weeks, in the darkened room. I was in high spirits. Valerie, paying her morning visit, seemed depressed.

"But think of it!" I cried in pardonable egotism. "To-morrow I shall be able to see you. I've longed for it as much as for the sight of the blue sky."

"There isn't any blue sky," said Valerie. "It's an inverted tureen that has held pea-soup."

Her voice had all the melancholy notes of the woodwind in the unseen shepherd's lament in "Tristan und Isolde."

"I don't know how to tell you," she exclaimed tragically, after a pause. "I shan't be here to-morrow. It's a bitter disappointment. My aunt in Wales is dying. I have been telegraphed for, and I must go."

She sat on the end of the couch where I was lounging, and took my hands.

"It isn't my fault."

My spirits fell headlong.

"I would just as soon keep blind," said I blankly.

"I thought you would say that."

A tear dropped on my hand. I felt that it was brutal of her aunt to make Valerie cry. Why could she not postpone her demise to a more suitable opportunity? I murmured, however, a few decent words of condolence.

"Thank you, Mr. Winter," said Valerie. "I am fond of my aunt; but I had set my heart on your seeing me. And she may not die for weeks and weeks! She was dying for ever so long last year, and got round again."

I ventured an arm about her shoulders, and spoke consolingly. The day would come when our eyes would meet. I called her Valerie and bade her address me as Harold.

I have come to the conclusion that the man who strikes out a new line in love-making is a genius.

"If I don't hurry I shall miss my train," she sighed at last.

She rose; I felt her bend over me. Her hands closed on my cheeks, and a kiss fluttered on my lips. I heard the light swish of her skirts and the quick opening and shutting of the door, and she was gone.

Valerie's aunt, like King Charles II, was an unconscionable time a-dying. When a note from Valerie announced her return to Grandchester, I had already gone blue-spectacled away. For some time I was not allowed to read or write, and during this period of probation urgent affairs summoned me to Vienna. Such letters as I wrote to Valerie had to be of the most elementary nature. If you have a heart of any capacity worth troubling about, you cannot empty it on one side of a sheet of notepaper. For mine reams would have been inadequate. I also longed to empty it in her presence, my eyes meeting hers for the first time. Thus, ever haunted by the beloved plain face and the memorable voice, I remained inarticulate.

As soon as my business was so far adjusted that I could leave Vienna, I started on a flying visit, post-haste, to England. The morning after my arrival beheld me in a railway carriage at Euston waiting for the train to carry me to Grandchester. I had telegraphed to Valerie; also to Mr. Deane, the oculist, for an appointment which might give colour to my visit. I was alone in the compartment. My thoughts, far away from the long platform, leaped the four hours that separated me from Grandchester. For the thousandth time I pictured our meeting. I foreshadowed speeches of burning eloquence. I saw the homely features transfigured. I closed my eyes the better to retain the beatific vision. The train began to move. Suddenly the door was opened, a girlish figure sprang into the compartment, and a porter running by the side of the train, threw in a bag and a bundle of wraps, and slammed the door violently. The young lady stood with her back to me, panting for breath. The luggage lay on the floor. I stooped to pick up the bag; so did the young lady. Our hands met as I lifted it to the rack.

"Oh, please, don't trouble!" she cried in a voice whose familiarity made my heart beat.

I caught sight of her face, for the first time, and my heart beat faster than ever. It was her face—the face that had dawned upon my blindness—the face I had grown to worship. I looked at her, transfixed with wonder. She settled herself unconcerned in the farther corner of the carriage. I took the opposite seat and leaned forward.

"You are Miss Deane?" I asked tremulously.

She drew herself up, on the defensive.

"That is my name," she said.

"Valerie!" I cried in exultation.

She half rose. "What right have you to address me?"

"I am Harold Winter," said I, taken aback by her outraged demeanour. "Is it possible that you don't recognize me?"

"I have never seen or heard of you before in my life," replied the young lady tartly, "and I hope you won't force me to take measures to protect myself against your impertinence."

I lay back against the cushions, gasping with dismay.

"I beg your pardon," said I, recovering; "I am neither going to molest you nor be intentionally impertinent. But, as your face has never been out of my mind for three months, and as I am travelling straight through from Vienna to Grandchester to see it for the first time, I may be excused for addressing you."

She glanced hurriedly at the communication-cord and then back at me, as if I were a lunatic.

"You are Miss Deane of Grandchester—daughter of Dr. Deane?" I asked.

"Yes."

"Valerie Deane, then?"

"I have told you so."

"Then all I can say is," I cried, losing my temper at her stony heartlessness, "that your conduct in turning an honest, decent man into a besotted fool, and then disclaiming all knowledge of him, is outrageous. It's damnable. The language hasn't a word to express it!"

She stood with her hand on the cord.

"I shall really have to call the guard," she said, regarding me coolly.

"You are quite free to do so," I answered. "But if you do, I shall have to show your letters, in sheer self-defence. I am not going to spend the day in a police-station."

She let go the cord and sat down again.

"What on earth do you mean?" she asked.

I took a bundle of letters from my pocket and tossed one over to her. She glanced at it quickly, started, as if in great surprise, and handed it back with a smile.

"I did not write that."

I thought I had never seen her equal for unblushing impudence. Her mellow tones made the mockery appear all the more diabolical.

"If you didn't write it," said I, "I should like to know who did."

"My Cousin Valerie."

"I don't understand," said I.

"My name is Valerie Deane and my cousin's name is Valerie Deane, and this is her handwriting."

Bewildered, I passed my hand over my eyes. What feline trick was she playing? Her treachery was incomprehensible.

"I suppose it was your Cousin Valerie who tended me during my blindness at your father's house, who shed tears because she had to leave me, who——"

"Quite possibly," she interrupted. "Only it would have been at her father's house and not mine. She does tend blind people, my father's patients."

I looked at her open-mouthed. "In the name of Heaven," I exclaimed, "Who are you, if not the daughter of Dr. Deane of Stavaton Street?"

"My father is Mr. Henry Deane, the oculist. You asked if I was the daughter of Dr. Deane. So many people give him the wrong title I didn't trouble to correct you."

It took me a few moments to recover. I had been making a

pretty fool of myself. I stammered out pleas for a thousand pardons. I confused myself, and her, in explanation. Then I remembered that the fathers were twin brothers and bore a strong resemblance one to the other. What more natural than that the daughters should also be alike?

"What I can't understand," said Miss Deane, "is how you mistook me for my cousin."

"Your voices are identical."

"But our outer semblances——"

"I have never seen your cousin—she left me before I recovered my sight."

"How then could you say you had my face before you for three months?"

"I am afraid, Miss Deane, I was wrong in that as in everything else. It was her face. I had a mental picture of it."

She put on a puzzled expression. "And you used the mental picture for the purpose of recognition?"

"Yes," said I.

"I give it up," said Miss Deane.

She did not press me further. Her Cousin Valerie's love affairs were grounds too delicate for her to tread upon. She turned the conversation by politely asking me how I had come to consult her father. I mentioned my friend Mobray and the gun accident. She remembered the case and claimed a slight acquaintance with Mobray, whom she had met at various houses in Grandchester. My credit as a sane and reputable person being established, we began to chat most amicably. I found Miss Deane an accomplished woman. We talked books, art, travel. She had the swift wit which delights in bridging the trivial and the great. She had a playful fancy. Never have I found a personality so immediately sympathetic. I told her a sad little Viennese story in which I happened to have played a minor part, and her tenderness was as spontaneous as Valerie's—my Valerie's. She had Valerie's woodland laugh. Were it not that her personal note, her touch on the strings of life differed essentially from my beloved's, I should have held it grotesquely impossible for any human being but Valerie to be sitting in the opposite corner of that railway carriage. Indeed there were moments when she was Valerie, when the girl waiting for me at Grandchester faded into the limbo of unreal things. A kiss from those lips had fluttered on mine. It were lunacy to doubt it.

During intervals of non-illusion I examined her face critically. There was no question of its unattractiveness to the casual observer. The nose was too large and fleshy, the teeth too prominent, the eyes too small. But my love had pierced to its underlying spirituality, and it was the face above all others that I desired.

Toward the end of a remarkably short four hours' journey, Miss Deane graciously expressed the hope that we might meet again.

"I shall ask Valerie," said I, "to present me in due form."

She smiled maliciously. "Are you quite sure you will be able to distinguish one from the other when my cousin and I are together?"

"Are you, then, so identically alike?"

"That's a woman's way of answering a question—by another question," she laughed.

"Well, but are you?" I persisted.

"How otherwise could you have mistaken me for her?" She had drawn off her gloves, so as to give a tidying touch to her hair. I noticed her hands, small, long, and deft. I wondered whether they resembled Valerie's.

"Would you do me the great favour of letting me touch your hand while I shut my eyes, as if I were blind?"

She held out her hand frankly. My fingers ran over it for a few seconds, as they had done many times over Valerie's. "Well?" she asked.

"Not the same," said I.

She flushed, it seemed angrily, and glanced down at her hand, on which she immediately proceeded to draw a glove.

"Yours are stronger. And finer," I added, when I saw that the tribute of strength did not please.

"It's the one little personal thing I am proud of," she remarked.

"You have made my four hours pass like four minutes," said I. "A service to a fellow-creature which you might take some pride in having performed."

"When I was a child I could have said the same of performing elephants."

"I am no longer a child, Miss Deane," said I with a bow.

What there was in this to make the blood rush to her pale cheeks I do not know. The ways of women have often surprised me. I have heard other men make a similar confession.

"I think most men are children," she said shortly.

"In what way?"

"Their sweet irresponsibility," said Miss Deane.

And then the train entered Grandchester Station.

I deposited my bag at the station hotel and drove straight to Stavaton Street. I forgot Miss Deane. My thoughts and longings centred in her beloved counterpart, with her tender, caressing ways, and just a subtle inflection in the voice that made it more exquisite than the voice to which I had been listening.

The servant who opened the door recognized me and smiled a welcome. Miss Valerie was in the drawing-room.

"I know the way," said I.

Impetuous, I ran up the stairs, burst into the drawing-room, and stopped short on the threshold in presence of a strange and exceedingly beautiful young woman. She was stately and slender. She had masses of bright brown hair waving over a beautiful brow. She had deep sapphire eyes, like stars. She had the complexion of a Greuze child. She had that air of fairy diaphaneity combined with the glow of superb health which makes the typical loveliness of the Englishwoman. I gaped for a second or two at this gracious apparition.

"I beg your pardon," said I; "I was told—"

The apparition who was standing by the fireplace smiled and came forward with extended hands.

"Why, Harold! Of course you were told. It is all right. I am Valerie."

I blinked; the world seemed upside down; the enchanting voice rang in my ears, but it harmonized in no way with the equally enchanting face. I put out my hand. "How do you do?" I said stupidly.

"But aren't you glad to see me?" asked the lovely young woman.

"Of course," said I; "I came from Vienna to see you."

"But you look disappointed."

"The fact is," I stammered, "I expected to see someone different—quite different. The face you described has been haunting me for three months."

She had the effrontery to laugh. Her eyes danced mischief.

"Did you really think me such a hideous fright?"

"You were not a fright at all," said I, remembering my late travelling companion.

And then in a flash I realised what she had done.

"Why on earth did you describe your cousin instead of yourself?"

"My cousin! How do you know that?"

"Never mind," I answered. "You did. During your description you had her face vividly before your mind. The picture was in some telepathic way transferred from your brain to mine, and there it remained. The proof is that when I saw a certain lady to-day I recognised her at once and greeted her effusively as Valerie. Her name did happen to be Valerie, and Valerie Deane too, and I ran the risk of a police-station—and I don't think it was fair of you. What prompted you to deceive me?"

I was hurt and angry, and I spoke with some acerbity. Valerie drew herself up with dignity.

"If you claim an explanation, I will give it to you. We have had young men patients in the house before, and, as they had nothing to do, they have amused themselves and annoyed me by falling in love with me. I was tired of it, and decided that it shouldn't happen in your case. So I gave a false description of myself. To make it consistent, I took a real person for a model."

"So you were fooling me all the time?" said I, gathering hat and stick.

Her face softened adorably. Her voice had the tones of the wood-wind.

"Not all the time, Harold," she said.

I laid down hat and stick.

"Then why did you not undeceive me afterward?"

"I thought," she said, blushing and giving me a fleeting glance, "well, I thought you—you wouldn't be sorry to find I wasn't—bad looking."

"I am sorry, Valerie," said I, "and that's the mischief of it."

"I was so looking forward to your seeing me," she said tearfully. And then, with sudden petulance, she stamped her small foot. "It is horrid of you—perfectly horrid—and I never want to speak to you again." The last word ended in a sob. She rushed to the door, pushed me aside, as I endeavoured to stop her, and fled in a passion of tears. *Spretæ injuria formæ*! Women have remained much the same since the days of Juno.

A miserable, remorseful, I wandered through the Grandchester streets, to keep my appointment with Mr. Henry Deane. After a short interview he dismissed me with a good report of my eyes. Miss Deane, dressed for walking, met me in the hall as the servant was showing me out, and we went together into the street.

"Well," she said with a touch of irony, "have you seen my cousin?"

"Yes," said I.

"Do you think her like me?"

"I wish to Heaven she were!" I exclaimed fervently. "I shouldn't be swirling round in a sort of maelstrom."

She looked steadily at me—I like her downrightness.

"Do you mind telling me what you mean?"

"I am in love with the personality of one woman and the face of another. And I never shall fall out of love with the face."

"And the personality?"

"God knows," I groaned.

"I never conceived it possible for any man to fall in love with a face so hopelessly unattractive," she said with a smile.

"It is beautiful," I cried.

She looked at me queerly for a few seconds, during which I had the sensation of something odd, uncanny having happened. I was fascinated. I found myself saying: "What did you mean by the 'sweet irresponsibility of man'?"

She put out her hand abruptly and said good-bye. I watched her disappear swiftly round a near corner, and I went, my head buzzing with her, back to my hotel. In the evening I dined with Dr. Deane. I had no opportunity of seeing Valerie alone. In a whisper she begged forgiveness. I relented. Her beauty and charm would have mollified a cross rhinoceros. The love in her splendid eyes would have warmed a snow image. The pressure of her hand at parting brought back the old Valerie, and I knew I loved her desperately. But inwardly I groaned, because she had not the face of my dreams. I hated her beauty. As soon as the front door closed behind me, my head began to buzz again with the other Valerie.

I lay awake all night. The two Valeries wove themselves inextricably together in my hopes and longings. I worshipped a composite chimera. When the grey dawn stole through my bedroom window, the chimera vanished, but a grey dubiety dawned upon my soul. Day invested it with a ghastly light. I rose a shivering wreck and fled from Grandchester by the first train.

I have not been back to Grandchester. I am in Vienna, whither I returned as fast as the Orient Express could carry me. I go to bed praying that night will dispel my doubt. I wake every morning to my adamantine indecision. That I am consuming away with love for one of the two Valeries is the only certain fact in my uncertain existence. But which of the Valeries it is I cannot for the life of me decide.

If any woman (it is beyond the wit of man) could solve my problem and save me from a hopeless and lifelong celibacy she would earn my undying gratitude.

IV

A WOMAN OF THE WAR

It was a tiny room at the top of what used to be a princely London mansion, the home of a great noble—a tiny room, eight feet by five, the sleeping-receptacle, in the good old days, for some unconsidered scullery-maid or under-footman. The walls were distempered and bare; the furniture consisted of a camp-bed, a chair, a deal chest of drawers, and a wash-stand—everything spotless. There was no fireplace. An aerial cell of a room, yet the woman in nurse's uniform who sat on the bed pressing her hands to burning eyes and aching brows thanked God for it. She thanked God for the privacy of it. Had she been a mere nurse, she would have had the third share of a large, comfortable bedroom, with a fire on bitter winter nights. But, as a Sister, she had a room to herself. Thank God she was alone! Coldly, stonily, silently alone.

The expected convoy of wounded officers had been late, and she had remained on duty beyond her hour, so as to lend a hand. Besides, she was not on the regular staff of the private hospital. She had broken a much needed rest from France to give temporary relief from pressure; so an extra hour or two did not matter.

The ambulances at length arrived. Some stretcher-cases, some walking. Among the latter was one, strongly knit, athletic, bandaged over the entire head and eyes, and led like a blind man by orderlies. When she first saw him in the vestibule, his humorous lips and resolute chin, which were all of his face unhidden, seemed curiously familiar; but during the bustle of installation, the half-flash of memory became extinct. It was only later, when she found that this head-bandaged man was assigned to her care, that she again took particular notice of him. Now that his overcoat had been taken off, she saw a major's crown on the sleeve of his tunic, and on the breast the ribbons of the D.S.O. and the M.C. He was talking to the matron.

"They did us proud all the way. Had an excellent dinner. It's awfully kind of you; but I want nothing more, I assure you, save just to get into bed and sleep like a dog."

And then she knew, in a sudden electric shock of certainty.

Half dazed, she heard the matron say,

"Sister, this is Major Shileto, of the Canadian army."

Half dazed, too, she took his gropingly outstretched hand. The gesture, wide of the mark, struck her with terror. She controlled herself. The matron consulted her typed return-sheet and ran off the medical statement of his injuries.

Major Shileto laughed.

"My hat! If I've got all that the matter with me, why didn't they bury me decently in France?"

She was rent by the gay laughter. When the matron turned away, she followed her.

"He isn't blind, is he?"

The matron, to whose naturally thin, pinched face worry and anxiety had added a touch of shrewishness, swung round on her.

"I thought you were a medical student. Is there anything about blindness here?" She smote the typed pages. "Of course not!"

The night staff being on duty, she had then fled the ward and mounted up the many stairs to the little room where she now sat, her hands to her eyes. Thank God he was not blind, and thank God she was alone!

But it had all happened a hundred years ago. Well, twenty years at least. In some vague period of folly before the war. Yet, after all, she was only five and twenty. When did it happen? She began an agonized calculation of dates——

She had striven almost successfully to put the miserable episode out of her mind, to regard that period of her life as a phase of a previous existence. Since the war began, carried on the flood-tide of absorbing work, she had had no time to moralize on the past. When it came before her in odd moments, she had sent it packing into the limbo of deformed and hateful things. And now the man with the gay laughter and the distinguished soldier's record had brought it all back, horribly vivid. For the scared moments, it was as though the revolutionary war-years had never been. She saw herself again the Camilla Warrington whom she had sought contemptuously to bury.

Had there been but a musk grain of beauty in that Camilla's story, she would have cherished the fragrance; but it had all been so ignoble and stupid. It had begun with her clever girlhood. The London University matriculation. The first bachelor-of-science degree. John Donovan, the great surgeon, a friend of her parents had encouraged her ambitions toward a medical career. She became a student at the Royal Free Hospital, of the consulting staff of which John Donovan was a member. For the first few months, all went well. She boarded nearby, in Bloomsbury, with a vague sort of aunt and distant cousins, folks of unimpeachable repute. Then, fired by the independent theories and habits of a couple of fellow students, she left the home of dull respectability and joined them in the slatternly bohemia of a Chelsea slum.

Oh, there was excuse for her youthful ardency to know all that there was to be known in the world at once! But if she had used her excellent brains, she would have realized that all that is to be known in the world could not be learned in her new environment. The unholy crew—they called it "The Brotherhood"—into which she plunged consisted of the dregs of a decadent art-world, unclean in person and in ethics. At first, she revolted. But the specious intellectuality of the crew fascinated her. Hitherto, she had seen life purely from the scientific angle. Material cause, material effect. On material life, art but an excrescence. She had been carelessly content to regard it merely as an interpretation of Beauty—to her, almost synonymous with prettiness.

At the various meeting-places of the crew, who talked with the interminability of a Russian Bolshevik, she learned a surprising lot of things about art that had never entered into her philosophy. She learned, or tried to learn—though her intelligence boggled fearfully at it—that the most vital thing in existence was the decomposition of phenomena, into interesting planes. All things in nature were in motion—as a scientific truth, she was inclined to accept the proposition; but the proclaimed fact that the representation of the Lucretian theory of fluidity by pictorial diagrams of intersecting planes was destined to revolutionize human society was beyond her comprehension. Still, it was vastly interesting. They got their plane-system into sculpture, into poetry, in some queer way into sociology.

A dingy young painter, meagerly hirsute, and a pallid young woman of anarchical politics assembled the crew one evening and, taking hands, announced the fact of their temporary marriage. The temporary bridegroom made a speech which was enthusiastically acclaimed. Their association was connected (so Camilla understood) with some sublime quality inherent in the intersecting planes. In these various pairings gleamed none of the old Latin Quarter joyousness. Their immorality was most austere.

To Camilla, it was all new and startling—a phantasmagorical world. Free love the merest commonplace. And, after a short while, into this poisonous atmosphere wherein she dwelt there came two influences. One was the vigilancy of the Women's Social and Political Union; the other, Harry Shileto, a young architect, a healthy man in the midst of an unhealthy tribe.

First, young Shileto. It is not that he differed much from the rest of the crew in crazy theory. He maintained, like everyone else, that Raphael and Brunelleschi had retarded the progress of the world for a thousand years; he despised Debussy for a half-hearted anarchist; he lamented the failure of the architectural iconoclasts of the late 'Nineties; his professed contempt for all human activities outside the pale of the slum was colossal; on the slum marriage-theory he was sound, nay, enthusiastic. But he was physically clean, physically good-looking, a man. And as Camilla, too, practised cleanliness of person, they were drawn together.

And, at the same time, the cold, relentless hand of the great feminist organization got her in its grip. Blindly acting under orders, she interrupted meetings, broke windows, went to prison, shrieked at street-corners the independence of her sex. And then she came down on the bed-rock of a sex by no means so independent—on the contrary, imperiously, tyrannically dependent on hers. The theories of the slum, uncompromisingly suffragist, were all very well; they might be practised with impunity by the anemic and slatternly; but when Harry Shileto entered into the quasi-marriage bond with Camilla, the instinct of the honest Briton clamored for the comforts of a home. As all the time that she could spare from the neglect of her studies at the hospital was devoted to feminist rioting, and a mere rag of a thing came back at night to the uncared-for flat, the young man rebelled.

"You can't love and look after me and fool about in prison at the same time. The two things don't hold together."

And Camilla, her nerves a jangle,

"I am neither your odalisk nor your housekeeper; so your remark does not apply."

Oh, the squalid squabbles! And then, at last,

"Camilla"—he gave her a letter to read—"I'm fed up with all this rot."

She glanced over the letter.

"Are you going to accept this post in Canada?" she asked sourly.

"Not if you promise to chuck the militant business and also these epicene freaks in Chelsea. I should like you to carry on at the hospital until you're qualified."

"You seem to forget," she said, "that I'm like a soldier under orders. If necessary, I must sacrifice my medical career. I also think your remarks about The Brotherhood simply beastly. I'll do no such thing."

Eventually it came to this:

"I don't care whether women get the vote or not. I think our Chelsea friends are the most pestilential set of rotors on the face of the earth. I've got my way to make in the world. Help me to do it. Let us get married in decent fashion and go out together."

"I being just the appanage of the rising young architect? Thank you for the insult."

And so the argument went on until he delivered his ultimatum:

"If I don't get a sensible message by twelve o'clock to-morrow at the club, I'll never see or hear of you as long as I live."

He went out of the flat. She sent no message. He did not return. After a while, a lawyer came and equitably adjusted joint financial responsibilities. And that was the end of the romance —if romance it could be termed. From that day to this, Harry Shileto had vanished from her ken.

His exit had been the end of the romance; but it had marked the beginning of tragedy. A man can love and, however justifiably, ride away—gloriously free. But the woman, for all her clamoring insistence, has to pay the debt from which man is physically exempt. Harry Shileto had already arrived in Canada when Camilla discovered the dismaying fact of her sex's disability. But her pride kept her silent, and of the child born in secret and dead within a fortnight, Harry Shileto never heard. Then, after a few months of dejection and loss of bearings and lassitude, the war thundered on the world. Her friend, John Donovan, the surgeon, was going out to France. She went to him and said: "I've wasted my time. It will take years for me to qualify. Let me go out and nurse." So, through his influence, she had stepped into the midst of the suffering of the war, and there she still remained and found great happiness in great work.

At length she drew her hands from her brow and went and poured out some water, for her throat was parched. On catching sight of herself in the mirror, she paused. She was pale and worn, and there were hollows beneath her eyes, catching shadows, but the war had not altogether marred her face. She took off her uniform-cap and revealed dark hair, full and glossy. She half wondered why the passage of a hundred years had not turned it white. Then she sat again on the bed and gripped her hands together.

"My God, what am I going to do?"

Had she loved him? She did not know. Her association with him could not have been entirely the callous execution of a social theory. There must have been irradiating gleams. Or had she wilfully excluded them from her soul? Once she had needed him and cried for him; but that was in an hour of weakness which she had conquered. And now, how could she face him? Still less, live in that terrible intimacy of patient and nurse? Oh, the miserable shame of it! All her womanhood shivered. Yet she must go through the ordeal. His bandaged eyes promised a short time of probation.

In the morning, after a restless night, she pulled herself together. After all, what need for such a commotion? If the three and a half years of war had not taught her dignity and self-reliance, she had learned but little.

There were four beds in the ward. Two on the right were occupied by officers, one with an arm-wound, another with a hole through his body. The third on the left by a pathetic-looking boy with a shattered knee, which, as the night Sister told her, gave him unceasing pain. The fourth by Major Shileto. To him she went first and whispered:

"I'm the day Sister. What kind of a night have you had?"

"Splendid!" His lips curled in a pleasant smile. "Just one long, beautiful blank."

"And the head?"

"Jammy. That's what it feels like. How it looks, I don't know."

"We'll see later when I do the dressings."

She went off to the boy. He also was a Canadian officer, and his name was Robin McKay. She lingered awhile in talk.

"Strikes me my military career is over, and I'll just have to hump around real estate in Winnipeg on a wooden leg."

"They aren't going to cut your leg off, you silly boy!" she laughed. "And what do you mean by 'humping round real estate?'"

"I'm a land surveyor. That's to say, my father is. See here:

When are they going to send me back? I'm afraid of this country."

"Why?"

"It's so lonesome. I don't know a soul."

"We'll fix that up all right for you," she said cheerily. "Don't worry."

The morning routine of the hospital began. In its appointed course came the time for dressings. Camilla, her nerves under control, went to Shileto.

"I've got to worry you, but I'll try to hurt as little as I can."

"Go ahead. Never mind me."

A probationer stood by, serving the laden wheel-table. At first, the symmetrically bandaged head seemed that of a thousand cases with which she had dealt. But when the crisp brown hair came to view, her hand trembled ever so little. She avoided touching it as far as was possible, for she remembered its feel. Dead, forgotten words rose lambent in her memory: "*It crackles like a cat's back. Let me see if there are sparks.*"

But in the midst of a great shaven patch there was a horrible scalp-wound which claimed her deftest skill. And she worked with steady fingers and uncovered the maimed brows and eyelids and cheekbones. How the sight had been preserved was a miracle. She cleansed the wounds with antiseptics and freed the eyelashes. She bent over him with deliberate intent.

"You can open your eyes for a second or two. You can see all right?"

"Rather. I can see your belt."

"Hold on, then."

With her swift craft, she blindfolded him anew, completed the bandaging, laid him back on his pillow, and went off with the probationer, wheeling the table to the other cases.

Later in the day, she was doing him some trivial service.

"What's the good of lying in bed all day?" he asked. "I want to get up and walk about."

"You've got a bit of a temperature."

"How much?"

"Ninety-nine point eight."

"Call that a temperature? I've gone about with a hundred and three."

"When was that?"

"When I first went out to Canada. I'm English, you know—only left the Old Country in Nineteen thirteen. But, when the war broke out, I joined up with the first batch of Canadians—lucky to start with a commission. Lord, it was hell's delight!"

"So I've been given to understand," said Camilla. "But what about your temperature of a hundred and three?"

"I was a young fool," said he, "and I didn't care what happened to me."

"Why?" she asked.

For a while he did not answer. He bit his lower lip, showing just a fine line of white teeth. Memory again clutched her. She was also struck by his unconscious realization of the aging quality of the war in that he spoke of his Nineteen-thirteen self as "a young fool." So far as that went, they thought in common.

Presently he said,

"Your voice reminds me of someone I used to know."

"Where?"

"Oh, here, in London."

She lied instinctively, with a laugh.

"It couldn't have been me. I've only just come to London—and I've never met Major Shileto before in my life."

"Of course not," he asserted readily. "But I had no idea two human voices could be so nearly identical."

"Still," she remarked, "you haven't told me of the temperature of a hundred and three."

"Oh, it is no story. Your voice brought it all back. You've heard of a man's own angry pride being cap and bells for a fool? Well"—he laughed apologetically—"it's idiotic. There's no point in it. I just went for about a week in a Canadian winter with that temperature—that's all."

"Because you couldn't bear to lie alone and think?"

"That's about it."

"Sister!" cried the boy, Robin McKay, from the next bed.

She obeyed the summons. What was the matter?

"Everything seems to have gotten mixed up, and my knees hurting like fury."

She attended to his crumpled bedclothes, cracked a little joke which made him laugh. Then the two other men claimed her notice. She carried on her work outwardly calm, smiling, self-reliant, the perfectly trained woman of the war. But her heart was beating in an unaccustomed way.

Her ministrations over, she left the ward for duty elsewhere.

At tea-time she returned, and aided the blindfolded man to get through the meal. The dread of the morning had given place to mingled mind-racking wonder and timidity. He had gone off, on the hot speed of their last quarrel, out of her life. Save for a short, anguished period, during which she had lost self-control, she had never reproached him. She had asserted her freedom. He had asserted his. Nay; more—he had held the door open for a way out from an impossible situation, and she had slammed the door in his face. Self-centered in those days, centered since the beginning of the war in human suffering, she had thought little of the man's feelings. He had gone away and forgotten, or done his best to forget, an ugly memory. Her last night's review of ghosts had proved the non-existence of any illusions among them. But now, now that the chances of war had brought them again together, the sound of her voice had conjured up in him, too, the ghosts of the past. She had been responsible for his going-about with a temperature of a hundred and three, and for his not caring what happened to him. He had lifted the corner of a curtain, revealing the possibility of undreamed-of happenings.

"You were quoting Tennyson just now," she remarked.

"Was I?"

"Your cap-and-bells speech."

"Oh, yes. What about it?"

"I was only wondering."

"Like a woman, you resent a half-confidence."

She drew in a sharp little breath. The words, the tone, stabbed her. She might have been talking to him in one of their pleasanter hours in the Chelsea flat. In spite of her burning curiosity, she said, "I'm not a woman; I'm a nurse."

"Since when?"

"As far as you are concerned, since September, '14, when I went out to France. I've been through everything—from the firing-line field-ambulances, casualty clearing-stations, base hospitals—and now I'm here having a rest-cure. Hundreds and hundreds of men have told me their troubles—so I've got to regard myself as a sort of mother confessor."

He smiled.

"Then, like a mother confessor, you resent a half-confidence?"

She put a cigarette between his lips and lit it for him.

"It all depends," she said lightly, "whether you want absolution or not. I suppose it's the same old story." She held her voice in command. "Every man thinks it's original. What kind of a woman was she?"

He parried the thrust.

"Isn't that rather too direct a question, even for a mother confessor?"

"You'll be spilling ash all over the bed. Here's an ash-tray." She guided his hand. "Then you don't want absolution?"

"Oh, yes, I do! But, you see, I'm not yet *in articulo mortis*, so I'll put off my confession."

"Anyhow, you loved the woman you treated badly?" The question was as casual as she could make it, while she settled the tea-things on the tray.

"It was a girl, not a woman."

"What has become of her?"

"That's what I should like to know."

"But you loved her?"

"Of course I did! I'm not a blackguard. Of course I loved her." Her pulse quickened. "But much water has run under London Bridge since then."

"And much blood has flowed in France."

"Everything—lives, habits, modes of thought have been

revolutionized. Yes"—he reflected for a moment—"it's odd how you have brought back old days. I fell in with a pestilential, so-called artistic crowd—I am an architect by profession—you know, men with long greasy hair and dirty fingernails and anarchical views. There was one chap especially, who I thought was decadent to the bone. Aloysius Eglington, he called himself." The man sprang vivid to her memory; he had once tried to make love to her. "Well, I came across him the other day with a couple of wound-stripes and the military-cross ribbon. For a man like that, what an upheaval!" He laughed again. "I suppose I've been a bit upheaved myself."

"I'm beginning to piece together your story of the temperature," she said pleasantly. "I suppose the girl was one of the young females of this anarchical crowd?"

Obviously the phrase jarred.

"I could never regard her in that light," he said coldly.

"The war has got hold of her, too, I suppose."

"No doubt. She was a medical student. May I have another cigarette?"

His tone signified the end of the topic. She smiled, for her putting-down was a triumph.

The probationer came up and took away the tea-tray. Camilla left her patient and went to the other beds.

That night again, she sat alone in her little white room and thought and thought. She had started the day with half-formed plans of flight before her identity could be discovered. She was there voluntarily, purely as an act of grace. She could walk out, without reproach, at a moment's notice. But now—had not the situation changed? To her, as to a stranger, he had confessed his love. She had not dared probe deeper—but might not a deeper probing have brought to light something abiding and beautiful? In the war, she had accomplished her womanhood. Proudly and rightly she recognized her development. He, too, had accomplished his manhood. And his dear face would be maimed and scarred for the rest of his life. Then, with the suddenness of a tropical storm, a wave of intolerable emotion surged through her. She uttered a little cry and broke into a passion of tears. And so her love was reborn.

Professional to the tips of her cool fingers, she dressed his wounds the next morning. But she did not lure him back across the years. The present held its own happiness, tremulous in its delicacy. It was he who questioned. Whereabouts in France had she been? She replied with scraps of anecdote. There was little of war's horror and peril through which she had not passed. She explained her present position in the hospital.

"By George, you're splendid!" he cried. "I wish I could have a look at you."

"You've lost your chance for to-day," she answered gaily. For she had completed the bandaging.

After dinner, she went out and walked the streets in a day-dream, a soft light in her eyes. The moment of recognition—and it was bound soon to come—could not fail in its touch of sanctification, its touch of beauty. He and she had passed through fires of hell and had emerged purified and tempered. They were clear-eyed, clear-souled. The greatest gift of God, miraculously regiven, they could not again despise. On that dreary afternoon, Oxford Street hummed with joy.

Only a freak of chance had hitherto preserved her anonymity. A reference by matron or probationer to Sister Warrington would betray her instantly. Should she await or anticipate betrayal?

In a fluttering tumult of indecision, she returned to the hospital. The visiting-hour had begun. When she had taken off her outdoor things, she looked into the ward. Around the two beds on the right, little groups of friends were stationed. The boy, Robin McKay, in the bed nearest the door on the left, caught sight of her and summoned her.

"Sister, come and pretend to be a visitor. There's not a soul in this country who could possibly come to see me. You don't know what it is to be homesick."

She sat by his side.

"All right. Imagine I'm an elderly maiden aunt from the country."

"You?" he cried, with overseas frankness. "You're only a kid yourself."

Major Shileto overheard and laughed. She blushed and half rose.

"That's not the way to treat visitors, Mr. McKay."

The boy stretched out his hand.

"I'm awfully sorry if I was rude. Don't go."

She yielded.

"All the same," she said, "you'll have to get used to a bit of loneliness. It can't be helped. Besides, you're not the only tiger that hasn't got a Christian. There's Major Shileto. And you can read and he can't."

The voice came from the next bed.

"Don't worry about me. Talk to the boy. I'll have someone to see me to-morrow. He won't, poor old chap!"

"Have a game of chess?" said the boy.

"With pleasure."

She fetched the board and chessmen from the long table running down the center of the ward, and they set out the pieces.

"I reckon to be rather good," said he. "Perhaps I might give you something."

"I'm rather good myself," she replied. "I was taught by—" She stopped short, on the brink of pronouncing the name of the young Polish master who lived (in a very material sense) on the fringe of the Chelsea crew. "We'll start even, at any rate."

They began. She realized that the boy had not boasted, and soon she became absorbed in the game. So intent was she on the problem presented by a brilliant and unexpected move on his part that she did not notice the opening of the door and the swift passage of a fur-coated figure behind her chair. It was a cry that startled her. A cry of surprise and joy, a cry of the heart.

"Marjorie!"

She looked up and saw the fur-coated figure—that of a girl with fair hair—on her knees by the bedside, and Harry Shileto's arms were round her and his lips to hers. She stared, frozen. She heard:

"I didn't expect you till to-morrow."

"I just had time to catch the train at Inverness. I've not brought an ounce of luggage. Oh, my poor, poor, old Harry!"

It was horrible.

The boy said:

"Never mind, Sister; he's got his Christian all right. Let's get on with the game."

Mechanically obeying a professional instinct, she looked at the swimming chess-board and made a move haphazard.

"I say—that won't do!" cried the boy. "It's mate for me in two moves. Buck up!"

With a great effort, she caught the vanishing tail of her previous calculation and made a move which happened to be correct.

"That's better," he said. "I hoped you wouldn't spot it. But I couldn't let you play the ass with your knight and spoil the game. Now, this demands deep consideration."

He lingered a while over his move. She looked across. The pair at the next bed were talking in whispers. The girl was now sitting on a chair by the bedside, and her back hid the face of the man, though her head was near his.

"There!" cried the boy triumphantly.

"I beg your pardon; I didn't see it."

"Oh, I say!" His finger indicated the move.

With half her brain at work, she moved a pawn a cautious step. The boy's whole heart was in his offensive. He swooped a bishop triumphantly athwart the board.

"There's only one thing can save you for mate in five moves. I know it isn't the proper thing to be chatting over chess, but I like it. I'm chatty by nature."

"Only one course open to save me from destruction?" she murmured.

"Just one."

And she heard, from the next bed:

"Are you sure, darling, you're only saying it to break the shock gently? Are you sure your eyes are alright?"

"Perfectly certain."

"I wish I could have real proof."

Camilla stared at the blankness of her vanished dream.

"Come along, Sister; put your back into it," chuckled Robin McKay.

She held her brows tight with her hands and strove to concentrate her tortured mind on the board. Her heart was in agony of desolation. The soft murmurings she could not but overhear pierced her brain. The poignant shame of her disillusionment burned her from head to foot. Again she heard the girl's pleading voice:

"Only for a minute. It couldn't hurt."

The boy said:

"Buck up. Just one tiny brain-wave."

At the end of her tether, she cried: "The only way out! I give it up!" and swept the pieces over the board.

She rose, stood transfixed with horror and sense of outrage. Harry Shileto, propped on pillows, was unwinding the bandages from his mangled head. Devils within her clamored for hysterical outcry. But something physical happened and checked the breath that was about to utter his Christian name. The boy had gripped her arm with all his young strength in passionate remonstrance.

"Oh, dear old thing—do play the game!"

"I'm sorry," she said, and he released her.

So she passed swiftly round the boy's bed to that of the foolish patient and arrested his hand.

"Major Shileto, what on earth are you doing?"

The girl, who was very pretty, turned on her an alarmed and tearful face.

"It was my fault, Sister. Oh, can I believe him?"

"You can believe me, at any rate," she replied with asperity, swiftly readjusting the bandage. "Major Shileto's sight is unaffected. But if I had not been here and he had succeeded in taking off his dressings, God knows what would have happened. Major Shileto, I put you on your honor not to do such a silly thing again."

"All right, Sister," he said, with a little shame-faced twitch of the lips. "*Parole d'officier.*"

The girl rose and drew her a step aside.

"Do forgive me, Sister. We have only been married five months—when he was last home on leave—and, you understand, don't you, what it would have meant to me if——"

"Of course I do. Anyhow, you can be perfectly reassured. But I must warn you," she whispered, and looked through narrowed eyelids into the girl's eyes; "he may be dreadfully disfigured."

The girl shrank terrified, but she cried,

"I hope I shall love him all the more for it!"

"I hope so, too," replied Camilla soberly. "I'll say good-bye," she added, in a louder tone, holding out her hand.

"I'll see you again to-morrow?" the girl asked politely.

"I'm afraid not."

"What's that?" cried Shileto.

"I told you I was only here as a bird of passage. My time's up to-day. Good-bye."

"I'm awfully sorry. Good-bye."

They shook hands. Camilla went to Robin McKay and bent over him.

"You're quite right, my dear boy. One ought to play the game to the bitter end. It's the thing most worth doing in life. God bless you!"

The boy stared wonderingly at her as she disappeared.

"I'm glad she's not going to be here any more," said the girl.

Her husband's lips smiled.

"Why?"

"She's a most heartless, overbearing woman."

"Oh, they all seem like that when they're upset," he laughed. "And I was really playing the most outrageous fool."

She put her head close to him and whispered,

"Don't you guess why I was so madly anxious to know that you could see?"

She told him. And, from that moment, the possessor of the remembered voice faded from his memory.

Camilla went to the matron.

"I'm sorry, but I've bitten off more than I can chew. If I go on an hour longer, I'll break down. I'm due in France in a fortnight, and I must have my rest."

"I can only thank you for your self-sacrificing help," said the matron.

But, four days later, ten days before her leave had expired, Camilla appeared at the casualty clearing-station in France of which she was a Sister-in-charge.

"What the devil are you here for?" asked the amazed commanding medical officer.

"England's too full of ghosts. They scared me back to realities."

The M.O. laughed to hide his inability to understand.

"Well, if you like 'em, it's all the same to me. I'm delighted to have you. But give me the good old ghosts of blighty all the time!"

The piercing of the line at Cambrai was a surprise no less to the Germans than to the British. The great tent of the casualty clearing-station was crammed with wounded. Doctors and nurses, with tense, burning eyes and bodies aching from strain, worked and worked, and thought nothing of that which might be passing outside. No one knew that the German wave had passed over. And the German wave itself, at that part of the line, was but a set of straggling and mystified groups.

Camilla Warrington, head of the heroic host of women working in the dimly lit reek of blood and agony, had not slept for two nights and two days. The last convoy of wounded had poured in a couple of hours before. She stood by the surgeon, aiding him, the perfect machine. At last, in the terrible rota, they came to a man swathed around the middle in the rough bandages of the field dressing-station. He was unconscious. They unwound him, and revealed a sight of unimaginable horror.

"He's no good, poor chap!" said the surgeon.

"Can't you try?" she asked, and put repressing hands on the wounded man.

"Not the slightest good," said the medical officer.

No one in the great tent of agony knew that they were isolated from the British army. From the outside, it looked solitary, lighted, and secure. Two German soldiers, casual stragglers, looked in at the door of the great tent. In the kindly German way, they each threw in a bomb, and ran off laughing. Seven men were killed outright and many rewounded. And Camilla Warrington was killed.[1]

[1] The bloody and hideous incident related

here is not an invention. It is true. It happened when and where I have indicated.—
W.J.L.

The guards, in their memorable sweep, cleared the ground. The casualty clearing-station again came into British hands.

There is a grave in that region whose head-board states that it is consecrated "to the Heroic Memory of Camilla Warrington, one of the Great Women of the War."

And Marjorie Shileto, to her husband healed and sound, searching like a foolish woman deep into his past history:

"It's awfully decent of you, darling, to hide nothing from me and to tell me about that girl in Chelsea. But what was she like?"

"My sweetheart," said he, like a foolish man, "she wasn't worth your little finger."

THE PRINCESS'S KINGDOM

That there was once a real Prince Rabomirski is beyond question. That he was Ottilie's father may be taken for granted. But that the Princess Rabomirski had a right to bear the title many folks were scandalously prepared to deny. It is true that when the news of the Prince's death reached Monte Carlo, the Princess, who was there at the time, showed various persons on whose indiscretion she could rely a holograph letter of condolence from the Tsar, and later unfolded to the amiable muddle-headed the intricacies of a lawsuit which she was instituting for the recovery of the estates in Poland; but her detractors roundly declared the holograph letter to be a forgery and the lawsuit a fiction of her crafty brain. Princess however she continued to style herself in Cosmopolis, and Princess she was styled by all and sundry. And little Ottilie Rabomirski was called the Princess Ottilie.

Among the people who joined heart and soul with the detractors was young Vince Somerset. If there was one person whom he despised and hated more than Count Bernheim (of the Holy Roman Empire) it was the Princess Rabomirski. In his eyes she was everything that a princess, a lady, a woman, and a mother should not be. She dressed ten years younger than was seemly, she spoke English like a barmaid and French like a cocotte, she gambled her way through Europe from year's end to year's end, and after neglecting Ottilie for twenty years, she was about to marry her to Bernheim. The last was the unforgivable offence.

The young man walked up and down the Casino Terrace of Illerville-sur-Mer, and poured into a friend's ear his flaming indignation. He was nine and twenty, and though he pursued the unpoetical avocation of sub-editing the foreign telegrams on a London daily newspaper, retained some of the vehemence of undergraduate days when he had chosen the career (now abandoned) of poet, artist, dramatist, and irreconcilable politician.

"Look at them!" he cried, indicating a couple seated at a distant table beneath the awning of the café. "Did you ever see anything so horrible in your life? The maiden and the Minotaur. When I heard of the engagement to-day I wouldn't believe it until she herself told me. She doesn't know the man's abomination. He's a by-word of reproach through Europe. His name stinks like his infernal body. The live air reeks with the scent he pours upon himself. There can be no turpitude under the sun in which the wretch doesn't wallow. Do you know that he killed his first wife? Oh, I don't mean that he cut her throat. That's far too primitive for such a complex hound. There are other ways of murdering a woman, my dear Ross. You kick her body and break her heart and defile her soul. That's what he did. And he has done it to other women."

"But, my dear man," remarked Ross, elderly and cynical, "he is colossally rich."

"Rich! Do you know where he made his money? In the cesspool of European finance. He's a Jew by race, a German by parentage, an Italian by upbringing and a Greek by profession. He has bucket-shops and low-down money-lenders' cribs and rotten companies all over the Continent. Do you remember Sequasto and Co.? That was Bernheim. England's too hot to hold him. Look at him now, he has taken off his hat. Do you know why he wears his greasy hair plastered over half his damned forehead? It's to hide the mark of the Beast. He's Antichrist! And when I think of that Jezebel from the Mile End Road putting Ottilie into his arms, it makes me see red. By heavens, it's touch and go that I don't slay the pair of them."

"Very likely they're not as bad as they're painted," said his friend.

"She couldn't be," Somerset retorted grimly.

Ross laughed, looked at his watch, and announced that it was time for *apéritifs*. The young man assented moodily, and they crossed the Terrace to the café tables beneath the awning. It was the dying afternoon of a sultry August day, and most of Illerville had deserted tennis courts, *tir aux pigeons* and other distractions to listen lazily to the band in the Casino shade. The place was crowded; not a table vacant. When the waiter at last brought one from the interior of the café, he dumped it down beside the table occupied by the unspeakable Bernheim and the little Princess Ottilie. Somerset raised his hat as he took his seat. Bernheim responded with elaborate politeness, and Princess Ottilie greeted him with a faint smile. The engaged pair spoke very little to each other. Bernheim lounged back in his chair smoking a cigar and looked out to sea with a bored expression. When the girl made a casual remark he nodded rudely without turning his head. Somerset felt an irresistible desire to kick him. His external appearance was of the type that irritated the young Englishman. He was too handsome in a hard, swaggering black-mustachioed way; he exaggerated to offence the English style of easy dress; he wore a too devil-may-care Panama, a too obtrusive coloured shirt and club tie; he wore no waistcoat, and the hem of his new flannel trousers, turned up six inches, disclosed a stretch of tan-coloured silk socks clocked with gold matching elegant tan shoes. He went about with a broken-spirited poodle. He was inordinately scented. Somerset glowered at him, and let his drink remain untasted.

Presently Bernheim summoned the waiter, paid him for the tea the girl had been drinking and pushed back his chair.

"This hole is getting on my nerves," he said in French to his companion. "I am going into the *circle* to play écarté. Will you go to your mother whom I see over there, or will you stay here?"

"I'll stay here," said the little Princess Ottilie.

Bernheim nodded and swaggered off. Somerset bent forward.

"I must see you alone to-night—quite alone. I must have you all to myself. How can you manage it?"

Ottilie looked at him anxiously. She was fair and innocent, of a prettiness more English than foreign, and the scare in her blue eyes made them all the more appealing to the young man.

"What is the good? You can't help me. Don't you see that it is all arranged?"

"I'll undertake to disarrange it at a moment's notice," said Somerset.

"Hush!" she whispered, glancing round; "somebody will hear. Everything is gossiped about in this place."

"Well, will you meet me?" the young man persisted.

"If I can," she sighed. "If they are both playing baccarat I may slip out for a little."

"As at Spa."

She smiled and a slight flush came into her cheek.

"Yes, as at Spa. Wait for me on the *plage* at the bottom of the Casino steps. Now I must go to my mother. She would not like to see me talking to you."

"The Princess hates me like poison. Do you know why?"

"No, and you are not going to tell me," she said demurely. "*Au revoir.*"

When she had passed out of earshot, Ross touched the young man's arm.

"I'm afraid, my dear Somerset, you are playing a particularly silly fool's game."

"Have you never played it?"

"Heaven forbid!"

"It would be a precious sight better for you if you had," growled Somerset.

"I'll take another quinquina," said Ross.

"Did you see the way in which the brute treated her?" Somerset exclaimed angrily. "If it's like that before marriage, what will it be after?"

"Plenty of money, separate establishments, perfect independence and happiness for each."

Somerset rose from the table.

"There are times, my good Ross," said he, "when I absolutely hate you."

Somerset had first met the Princess Rabomirski and her daughter three years before, at Spa. They were staying at the same hotel, a very modest one which, to Somerset's mind, ill-accorded with the Princess's pretensions. Bernheim was also in attendance, but he disposed his valet, his motor-car, and himself in the luxurious Hôtel d'Orange, as befitted a man of his quality; also he was in attendance not on Ottilie, but on the Princess, who at that time was three years younger and a trifle less painted. Now, at Illerville-sur-Mer the trio were stopping at the Hotel Splendide, a sumptuous hostelry where season prices were far above Somerset's moderate means. He contented himself with the little hotel next door, and hated the Hotel Splendide and all that it contained, save Ottilie, with all his heart. But at Spa, the Princess was evidently in low water from which she did not seem to be rescued by her varying luck at the tables. Ottilie was then a child of seventeen, and Somerset was less attracted by her delicate beauty than by her extraordinary loneliness. Day after day, night after night he would come upon her sitting solitary on one of the settees in the gaming-rooms, like a forgotten fan or flower, or wandering wistfully from table to table, idly watching the revolving wheels. Sometimes she would pause behind her mother's or Bernheim's chair to watch their game; but the Princess called her a little *porte-malheur* and would drive her away. In the mornings, or on other rare occasions, when the elder inseparables were not playing roulette, Ottilie hovered round them at a distance, as disregarded as a shadow that followed them in space of less dimensions, as it were, wherever they went. In the Casino rooms, if men spoke to her, she replied in shy monosyllables and shrank away. Somerset who had made regular acquaintance with the Princess at the hotel and taken a chivalrous pity on the girl's loneliness, she admitted first to a timid friendship, and then to a childlike intimacy. Her face would brighten and her heartbeat a little faster when she saw his young, well-knit figure appear in the distance; for she knew he would come straight to her and take her from the hot room, heavy with perfumes and tobacco, on to the cool balcony, and talk of all manner of pleasant things. And Somerset found in this neglected, little sham Princess what his youth was pleased to designate a flower-like soul. Those were idyllic hours. The Princess, glad to get the embarrassing child out of the way, took no notice of the intimacy. Somerset fell in love.

It lasted out a three-years' separation, during which he did not hear from her. He had written to several addresses, but a cold Post Office returned his letters undelivered, and his only consolation was to piece together from various sources the unedifying histories of the Princess Rabomirski and the Count Bernheim of the Holy Roman Empire. He came to Illerville-sur-Mer for an August holiday. The first thing he did when shown into his hotel bedroom was to gaze out of window at the beach and the sea. The first person his eyes rested upon was the little Princess Ottilie issuing, alone as usual, from the doors of the next hotel.

He had been at Illerville a fortnight—a fortnight of painful joy. Things had changed. Their interviews had been mostly stolen, for the Princess Rabomirski had rudely declined to renew the acquaintance and had forbidden Ottilie to speak to him. The girl, though apparently as much neglected as ever, was guarded against him with peculiar ingenuity. Somerset, aware that Ottilie, now grown from a child into an exquisitely beautiful and marriageable young woman, was destined by a hardened sinner like the Princess for a wealthier husband than a poor newspaper man with no particular prospects, could not, however, quite understand the reasons for the virulent hatred of which he was the object. He overheard the Princess one day cursing her daughter in execrable German for having acknowledged his bow a short time before. Their only undisturbed time together was in the sea during the bathing hour. The Princess, hating the pebbly beach which cut to pieces her high-heeled shoes, never watched the bathers; and Bernheim did not bathe (Somerset, prejudiced, declared that he did not even wash) but remained in his bedroom till the hour of *déjeuner*. Ottilie, attended only by her maid, came down to the water's edge, threw off her *peignoir*, and, plunging into the water, found Somerset waiting.

Now Somerset was a strong swimmer. Moderately proficient at all games as a boy and an undergraduate, he had found that swimming was the only sport in which he excelled, and he had cultivated and maintained the art. Oddly enough, the little Princess Ottilie, in spite of her apparent fragility, was also an excellent and fearless swimmer. She had another queer delight for a creature so daintily feminine, the *salle d'armes*, so that the muscles of her young limbs were firm and well ordered. But the sea was her passion. If an additional bond between Somerset and herself were needed it would have been this. Yet, though it is a pleasant thing to swim far away into the loneliness of the sea with the object of one's affections, the conditions do not encourage sustained conversation on subjects of vital interest. On the day when Somerset learned that his little princess was engaged to Bernheim he burned to tell her more than could be spluttered out in ten fathoms of water. So he urged her to an assignation.

At half-past ten she joined him at the bottom of the Casino steps. The shingly beach was deserted, but on the terrace above the throng was great, owing to the breathless heat of the night.

"Thank Heaven you have come," said he. "Do you know how I have longed for you?"

She glanced up wistfully into his face. In her simple cream dress and burnt straw hat adorned with white roses around the brim, she looked very fair and childlike.

"You mustn't say such things," she whispered. "They are wrong now. I am engaged to be married."

"I won't hear of it," said Somerset. "It is a horrible nightmare —your engagement. Don't you know that I love you? I loved you the first minute I set my eyes on you at Spa."

Princess Ottilie sighed, and they walked along the boards behind the bathing-machines, and down the rattling beach to the shelter of a fishing boat, where they sat down, screened from the world with the murmuring sea in front of them. Somerset talked of his love and the hatefulness of Bernheim. The little Princess sighed again.

"I have worse news still," she said. "It will pain you. We are going to Paris to-morrow, and then on to Aix-les-Bains. They have just decided. They say the baccarat here is silly, and they might as well play for bon-bons. So we must say good-bye to-night—and it will be good-bye for always."

"I will come to Aix-les-Bains," said Somerset.

"No—no," she answered quickly. "It would only bring trouble on me and do no good. We must part to-night. Don't you think it hurts me?"

"But you must love me," said Somerset.

"I do," she said simply, "and that is why it hurts. Now I must be going back."

"Ottilie," said Somerset, grasping her hands: "Need you ever go back?"

"What do you mean?" he asked.

"Come away from this hateful place with me—now, this minute. You need never see Bernheim again as long as you live. Listen. My friend Ross has a motor-car. I can manage it—so there will be only us two. Run into your hotel for a thick cloak, and meet me as quickly as you can behind the tennis-courts. If we go full speed we'll catch the night-boat at Dieppe. It will be a wild race for our life happiness. Come."

In his excitement he rose and pulled her to her feet. They faced each other for a few glorious moments, panting for breath, and then Princess Ottilie broke down and cried bitterly.

"I can't dear, I can't. I must marry Bernheim. It is to save my mother from something dreadful. I don't know what it is—but she went on her knees to me, and I promised."

"If there's a woman in Europe capable of getting out of her difficulties unaided it is the Princess Rabomirski," said Somerset. "I am not going to let you be sold. You are mine, Ottilie, and by Heaven, I'm going to have you. Come."

He urged, he pleaded, he put his strong arms around her as if he would carry her away bodily. He did everything that a frantic young man could do. But the more the little Princess wept, the more inflexible she became. Somerset had not realized before this steel in her nature. Raging and vehemently urging he accompanied her back to the Casino steps.

"Would you like to say good-bye to me to-morrow morning, instead of to-night?" she asked, holding out her hand.

"I am never going to say good-bye," cried Somerset.

"I shall slip out to-morrow morning for a last swim—at six o'clock," she said, unheeding his exclamation. "Our train goes at ten." Then she came very close to him.

"Vince dear, if you love me, don't make me more unhappy than I am."

It was an appeal to his chivalry. He kissed her hand, and said:

"At six o'clock."

But Somerset had no intention of bidding her a final farewell in the morning. If he followed her the world over he would snatch her out of the arms of the accursed Bernheim and marry her by main force. As for the foreign telegrams of *The Daily Post*, he cared not how they would be sub-edited. He went to bed with lofty disregard of Fleet Street and bread and butter. As for the shame from which Ottilie's marriage would save her sainted mother, he did not believe a word of it. She was selling Ottilie to Bernheim for cash down. He stayed awake most of the night plotting schemes for the rescue of his Princess. It would be an excellent plan to insult Bernheim and slay him outright in a duel. Its disadvantages lay in his own imperfections as a duellist, and for the first time he cursed the benign laws of his country. At length he fell asleep; woke up to find it daylight, and leaped to his feet in a horrible scare. But a sight of his watch reassured him. It was only five o'clock. At half-past he put on a set of bathing things and sat down by the window to watch the hall door of the Hotel Splendide. At six, out came the familiar figure of the little Princess, draped in her white *peignoir*. She glanced up at Somerset's window. He waved his hand, and in a minute or two they were standing side by side at the water's edge. It was far away from the regular bathing-place marked by the bathing cabins, and further still from the fishing end of the beach where alone at that early hour were signs of life visible. The town behind them slept in warmth and light. The sea stretched out blue before them unrippled in the still air. A little bank of purple cloud on the horizon presaged a burning day.

The little Princess dropped her *peignoir* and kicked off her straw-soled shoes, and gave her hand to her companion. He glanced at the little white feet which he was tempted to fall down and kiss, and then at the wistful face below the blue-silk foulard knotted in front over the bathing-cap. His heart leaped at her bewildering sweetness. She was the morning incarnate.

She read his eyes and flushed pink.

"Let us go in," she said.

They waded in together, hand-in-hand, until they were waist deep. Then they struck out, making for the open sea. The sting of the night had already passed from the water. To their young blood it felt warm. They swam near together, Ottilie using a steady breast stroke and Somerset a side stroke, so that he could look at her flushed and glistening face. From the blue of the sea and the blue of the sky to the light blue of the silk foulard, the blue of her eyes grew magically deep.

"There seems to be nothing but you and me in God's universe, Ottilie," said he. She smiled at him. He drew quite close to her.

"If we could only go on straight until we found an enchanted island which we could have as our kingdom."

"The sea must be our kingdom," said Ottilie.

"Or its depths. Shall we dive down and look for the 'ceiling of amber, the pavement of pearl,' and the 'red gold throne in the heart of the sea' for the two of us?"

"We should be happier than in the world," replied the little Princess.

They swam on slowly, dreamily, in silence. The mild waves lapped against their ears and their mouths. The morning sun lay at their backs, and its radiance fell athwart the bay. Through the stillness came the faint echo of a fisherman on the far beach hammering at his boat. Beyond that and the gentle swirl of the water there was no sound. After a while they altered their course so as to reach a small boat that lay at anchor for the convenience of the stronger swimmers. They clambered up and sat on the gunwale, their feet dangling in the sea.

"Is my princess tired?" he asked.

She laughed in merry scorn.

"Tired? Why, I could swim twenty times as far. Do you think I have no muscle? Feel. Don't you know I fence all the winter?"

She braced her bare arm. He felt the muscle; then, relaxing it, by drawing down her wrist, he kissed it very gently.

"Soft and strong—like yourself," said he. Ottilie said nothing, but looked at her white feet through the transparent water. She thought that in letting him kiss her arm and feeling as though he had kissed right through to her heart, she was exhibiting a pitiful lack of strength. Somerset looked at her askance, uncertain. For nothing in the world would he have offended.

"Did you mind?" he whispered.

She shook her head and continued to look at her feet. Somerset felt a great happiness pulse through him.

"If I gave you up," said he, "I should be the poorest spirited dog that ever whined."

"Hush!" she said, putting her hand in his. "Let us think only of the present happiness."

They sat silent for a moment, contemplating the little red-roofed town and Illerville-sur-Mer, which nestled in greenery beyond the white sweep of the beach, and the rococo hotels and the casino, whose cupolas flashed gaudily in the morning sun. From the north-eastern end of the bay stretched a long line of sheer white cliff as far as the eye could reach. Towards the west it was bounded by a narrow headland running far out to sea.

"It looks like a frivolous little Garden of Eden," said Somerset, "but I wish we could never set foot in it again."

"Let us dive in and forget it," said Ottilie.

She slipped into the water. Somerset stood on the gunwale and dived. When he came up and had shaken the salt water from his nostrils, he joined her in two or three strokes.

"Let us go round the point to the little beach the other side."

She hesitated. It would take a long time to swim there, rest, and swim back. Her absence might be noticed. But she felt reckless. Let her drink this hour of happiness to the full. What mattered anything that could follow? She smiled assent, and they struck out steadily for the point. It was good to have the salt smell and the taste of the brine and the pleasant smart of the eyes; and to feel their mastery of the sea. As they threw out their flashing white arms and topped each tiny wave they smiled in exultation. To them it seemed impossible that any-one could drown. For the buoyant hour they were creatures of the element. Now and then a gull circled before them, looked at them unconcerned, as if they were in some way his kindred, and swept off into the distance. A tired white butterfly settled for a moment on Ottilie's head; then light-heartedly fluttered away sea-wards to its doom. They swam on and on, and they neared the point. They slackened for a moment, and he brought his face close to hers.

"If I said 'Let us swim on for ever and ever,' would you do it?"

"Yes," she said, looking deep into his eyes.

After a while they floated restfully. The last question and answer seemed to have brought them a great peace. They were conscious of little save the mystery of the cloudless ether above their faces and the infinite sea that murmured in their ears strange harmonies of Love and Death—harmonies woven from the human yearnings of every shore and the hushed secrets of eternal time. So close were they bodily together that now and then hand touched hand and limb brushed limb. A happy stillness of the soul spread its wings over them and they felt it to be a consecration of their love. Presently his arm sought her, encircled her, brought her head on his shoulder.

"Rest a little," he whispered.

She closed her eyes, surrendered her innocent self to the flooding rapture of the moment. The horrors that awaited her passed from her brain. He had come to the lonely child like a god out of heaven. He had come to the frightened girl like a new terror. He was by her side now, the man whom of all men God had made to accomplish her womanhood and to take all of soul and body, sense and brain that she had to give. Their salt lips met in a first kiss. Words would have broken the spell of the enchantment cast over them by the infinite spaces of sea and sky. They drifted on and on, the subtle, subconscious movement of foot and hand keeping them afloat. The little Princess moved closer to him so as to feel more secure around her the circling pressure of his arm. He laughed a man's short, exultant laugh, and gripped her more tightly. Never had he felt his strength more sure. His right arm and his legs beat rhythmically and he felt the pulsation of the measured strokes of his companion's feet and the water swirled past his head, so that he knew they were making way most swiftly. Of exertion there was no sense whatever. He met her eyes fixed through half-shut lids upon his face.

Her soft young body melted into his. He lost count of time and space. Now and then a little wave broke over their faces, and they laughed and cleared the brine from their mouths and drew more close together.

"If it wasn't for that," she whispered once, "I could go to sleep."

Soon they felt the gentle rocking of the sea increase and waves broke more often over them. Somerset was the first to note the change. Loosening his hold of Ottilie, he trod water and looked around. To his amazement they were still abreast of the point, but far out to sea. He gazed at it uncomprehendingly for an instant, and then a sudden recollection smote him like a message of death. They had caught the edge of the current against which swimmers were warned, and the current held them in its grip and was sweeping them on while they floated foolishly. A swift glance at Ottilie showed him that she too realized the peril. With the outcoming tide it was almost impossible to reach the shore.

"Are you afraid?" he asked.

She shook her head. "Not with you."

He scanned the land and the sea. On the arc of their horizon lay the black hull of a tramp steamer going eastwards. Far away to the west was a speck of white and against the pale sky a film of smoke. Landwards beyond the shimmering water stretched the sunny bay of the casino. Its gilt cupolas shot tiny flames. The green-topped point, its hither side deep in shadow, reached out helplessly for them. Somerset and Ottilie still paused, doing nothing more than keeping themselves afloat, and they felt the current drifting them ever seawards.

"It looks like death," he said gravely. "Are you afraid to die?"

Again Ottilie said, "Not with you."

He looked at the land, and he looked at the white speck

and the puff of smoke. Then suddenly his heart leaped with the thrilling inspiration of a wild impossibility.

"Let us leave Illerville and France behind us. Death is as certain either way."

The little Princess looked at him wonderingly.

"Where are we going?"

"To England."

"Anywhere but Illerville," she said.

He struck out seawards, she followed. Each saw the other's face white and set. They had current and tide with them, they swam steadily, undistressed. After a silence she called to him.

"Vince, if we go to our kingdom under the sea, you will take me down in your arms?"

"In a last kiss," he said.

He had heard (as who has not) of Love being stronger than Death. Now he knew its truth. But he swore to himself a great oath that they should not die.

"I shall take my princess to a better kingdom," he said later.

Presently he heard her breathing painfully. She could not hold out much longer.

"I will carry you," he said.

An expert swimmer, she knew the way to hold his shoulders and leave his arms unimpeded. The contact of her light young form against his body thrilled him and redoubled his strength. He held his head for a second high out of the water and turned half round.

"Do you think I am going to let you die—now?"

The white speck had grown into a white hull, and Somerset was making across its track. To do so he must deflect slightly from the line of the current. His great battle began.

He swam doggedly, steadily, husbanding his strength. If the vessel justified his first flash of inspiration, and if he could reach her, he knew how he should act. As best he could, for it was no time for speech, he told Ottilie his hopes. He felt the spray from her lips upon his cheek, as she said:

"It seems sinful to wish for greater happiness than this."

After that there was utter silence between them. At first he thought exultingly of Bernheim and the Princess Rabomirski, and the rage of their wicked hearts; of the future glorified by his little Princess of the unconquerable soul: of the present's mystic consummation of their marriage. But gradually mental concepts lost sharpness of definition. Sensation began to merge itself into a half-consciousness of stroke on stroke through the illimitable waste. Despite the laughing morning sunshine, the sky became dark and lowering. The weight on his neck grew heavier. At first Ottilie had only rested her arms. Now her feet were as lead and sank behind him; her clasp tightened about his shoulders. He struggled on through a welter of sea and mist. Strange sounds sang in his ears, as if over them had been clamped great sea-shells. At each short breath his throat gulped down bitter water. A horrible pain crept across his chest. His limbs seemed paralysed and yet he remained above the surface. The benumbed brain wondered at the miracle....

The universe broke upon his vision as a blurred mass of green and white. He recognised it vaguely as his kingdom beneath the sea, and as in a dream he remembered his promise. He slipped round. His lips met Ottilie's. His arms wound round about her, and he sank, holding her tightly clasped.

Strange things happened. He was pulled hither and thither by sea monsters welcoming him to his kingdom. In a confused way he wondered that he could breathe so freely in the depths of the ocean. Unutterable happiness stole upon him. The Kingdom was *real*. His sham Princess would be queen in very truth. But where was she?

He opened his eyes and found himself lying on the deck of a ship. A couple of men were doing funny things to his arms. A rosy-faced man in white ducks and a yachting cap stood over him with a glass of brandy. When he had drunk the spirit, the rosy man laughed.

"That was a narrow shave. We got you just in time. We were nearly right on you. The young woman is doing well. My wife is looking after her."

As soon as he could collect his faculties, Somerset asked,

"Are you the *Mavis*?"

"Yes."

"I felt sure of it. Are you Sir Henry Ransome?"

"That's my name."

"I heard you were expected at Illerville to-day," said Somerset. "That is why I made for you."

The two men who had been doing queer things with his arms wrapped him in a blanket and propped him up against the deck cabin.

"But what on earth were you two young people doing in the middle of the English Channel?" asked the owner of the *Mavis*.

"We were eloping," said Somerset.

The other looked at him for a bewildered moment and burst into a roar of laughter. He turned to the cabin door and disappeared, to emerge a moment afterwards followed by a lady in a morning wrapper.

"What do you think, Marian? It's an elopement."

Somerset smiled at them.

"Have you ever heard of the Princess Rabomirski? You have? Well, this is her daughter. Perhaps you know of the Count Bernheim who is always about with the Princess?"

"I trod on him last winter at Monte Carlo," said Sir Henry Ransome.

"He survives," said Somerset, "and has bought the Princess Ottilie from her mother. He's not going to get her. She belongs to me. My name is Somerset, and I am foreign sub-editor of the *Daily Post.*"

"I am very pleased to make your acquaintance, Mr. Somerset," said Sir Henry with a smile. "And now what can I do for you?"

"If you can lend us some clothes and take us to any part on earth save Illerville-sur-Mer, you will earn our eternal gratitude."

Sir Henry looked doubtful. "We have made our arrangements for Illerville," said he.

His wife broke in.

"If you don't take these romantic beings straight to Southampton, I'll never set my foot upon this yacht again."

"It was you, my dear, who were crazy to come to Illerville."

"Don't you think," said Lady Ransome, "you might provide Mr. Somerset with some dry things?"

Four hours afterwards Somerset sat on deck by the side of Ottilie, who, warmly wrapped, lay on a long chair. He pointed to the far-away coastline of the Isle of Wight.

"Behold our kingdom!" said he.

The little Princess laughed.

"That is not our kingdom."

"Well, what is?"

"Just the little bit of space that contains both you and me," she said.

THE HEART AT TWENTY

The girl stood at the end of the little stone jetty, her hair and the ends of her cheap fur boa and her skirts all fluttering behind her in the stiff north-east gale. Why anyone should choose to stand on the jetty on a raw December afternoon with the wind in one's teeth was a difficult problem for a comfort-loving, elderly man like myself, and I pondered over it as I descended the slope leading from the village to the sea. It was nothing, thought I, but youth's animal delight in physical things. A few steps, however, brought me in view of her face in half-profile, and I saw that she did not notice wind or spray, but was staring out to sea with an intolerable wistfulness. A quick turn in the path made me lose the profile. I crossed the road that ran along the shore and walked rapidly along the jetty. Arriving within hailing distance I called her.

"Pauline."

She pivoted round like a weather-cock in a gust and with a sharp cry leapt forward to meet me. Her face was aflame with great hope and joy. I have seen to my gladness that expression once before worn by a woman. But as soon as this one recognised me, the joy vanished, killed outright.

"Oh, it's you," she said, with a quivering lip.

"I am sorry, my dear," said I, taking her hand. "I can't help it. I wish from my heart I were somebody else."

She burst into tears. I put my arm around her and drew her to me, and patted her and said, "There, there!" in the blundering masculine way. Having helped to bring her into the world twenty years before, I could claim fatherly privileges.

"Oh, Doctor," she sobbed, dabbing her pretty young eyes with a handkerchief. "Do forgive me. Of course I am glad to see you. It was the shock. I thought you were a ghost. No one ever comes to Ravetot."

"Never?" I asked mildly.

The tears flowed afresh. I leaned against the parapet of the jetty for comfort's sake, and looked around me. Ravetot-sur-Mer was not the place to attract visitors in December. A shingle beach with a few fishing-boats hauled out of reach of the surf; a miniature casino, like an impudently large summer-house, shuttered-up, weather-beaten and desolate; a weather-beaten, desolate, and shuttered-up Hôtel de l'Univers, and a perky deserted villa or two on the embankment; a cliff behind them, topped by a little grey church; the road that led up the gorge losing itself in the turn—and that was all that was visible of Ravetot-sur-Mer. A projecting cliff bounded the bay at each side, and in front seethed the grey, angry Channel. It was an Aceldama of a spot in winter; and only a matter of peculiar urgency had brought me hither. Pauline and her decrepit rascal of a father were tied to Ravetot by sheer poverty. He owned a pretty villa half a mile inland, and the rent he obtained for it during the summer enabled them to live in some miraculous way the rest of the year. They, the Curé and the fisher-folk, were the sole winter inhabitants of the place. The nearest doctor lived at Merville, twenty kilometres away, and there was not even an educated farmer in the neighbourhood. Yet I could not help thinking that my little friend's last remark was somewhat disingenuous.

"Are you quite sure, my dear," I said, "that no one ever comes to Ravetot?"

"Has father told you?" she asked tonelessly.

"No. I guessed it. I have extraordinary powers of divination. And somebody has been making my little girl miserable."

"He has broken my heart," said Pauline.

I pulled the collar of my fur-lined coat above my ears which the north-east wind was biting. Being elderly and heart-whole I am sensitive to cold. I proposed that we should walk up and down the jetty while she told me her troubles, and I hooked her arm in mine.

"Who was he?" I asked. "And what was he doing here?"

"Oh, Doctor! what does it matter?" she answered tearfully. "I never want to see him again."

"Don't fib," said I. "If the confounded blackguard were here now——"

"But he isn't a blackguard!" she flashed. "If he were I shouldn't be so miserable. I should forget him. He is good and kind, and noble, and everything that is right. I couldn't have expected him to act otherwise—it was awful, horrible—and when you called me by name I thought it was he——"

"And the contradictious feminine did very much want to see him?" said I.

"I suppose so," she confessed.

I looked down at her pretty face and saw that it was wan and pinched.

"You have been eating little and sleeping less. For how long?" I demanded sternly.

"For a week," she said pitifully.

"We must change all that. This abominable hole is a kind of

cold storage for depression."

She drew my arm tighter. She had always been an affectionate little girl, and now she seemed to crave human sympathy and companionship.

"I don't mind it now. It doesn't in the least matter where I am. Before he came, I used to hate Ravetot, and long for the gaiety and brightness of the great world. I used to stand here for hours and just long and long for something to happen to take us away; and it seemed no good. Here I was for the rest of time —with nothing to do day after day but housework and sewing and reading, while father sat by the fire, with his little roulette machine and Monte Carlo averages and paper and pencil, working out the wonderful system that is going to make our fortune. We'll never have enough money to go to Monte Carlo for him to try it, so that is some comfort. One would have thought he had had enough of gambling."

She made the allusion, very simply, to me—an old friend. Her father had gambled away a fortune, and in desperation had forged another man's name on the back of a bill, for which he had suffered a term of imprisonment. His relatives had cast him out. That was why he lived in poverty-stricken seclusion at Ravetot-sur-Mer. He was not an estimable old man, and I had always pitied Pauline for being so parented. Her mother had died years ago. I thought I would avoid the painful topic.

"And so," said I, after we had gone the length of the jetty in silence and had turned again, "one day when the lonely little princess was staring out to sea and longing for she knew not what, the young prince out of the fairy tale came riding up behind her —and stayed just long enough to make her lose her heart—and then rode off again."

"Something like it—only worse," she murmured. And then, with a sudden break in her voice, "I will tell you all about it. I shall go mad if I don't. I haven't a soul in the world to speak to. Yes. He came. He found me standing at the end of the jetty. He asked his way, in French, to the cemetery, and I recognised from his accent that he was English like myself. I asked him why he wanted to go to the cemetery. He said that it was to see his wife's grave. The only Englishwoman buried here was a Mrs. Everest, who was drowned last summer. This was the husband. He explained that he was in the Indian Civil Service, was now on leave. Being in Paris he thought he would like to come to Ravetot, where he could have quiet, in order to write a book."

"I understood it was to see his wife's grave," I remarked.

"He wanted to do that as well. You see, they had been separated for some years—judicially separated. She was not a nice woman. He didn't tell me so; he was too chivalrous a gentleman. But I had learned about her from the gossip of the place. I walked with him to the cemetery. I know a well-brought-up girl wouldn't have gone off like that with a stranger."

"My dear," said I, "in Ravetot-sur-Mer she would have gone off with a hippogriffin."

She pressed my arm. "How understanding you are, doctor, dear."

"I have an inkling of the laws that govern humanity," I replied. "Well, and after the pleasant trip to the cemetery?"

"He asked me whether the café at the top of the hill was really the only place to stay at in Ravetot. It's dreadful, you know—no one goes there but fishermen and farm labourers—and it is the only place. The hotel is shut up out of the season. I said that Ravetot didn't encourage visitors during the winter. He looked disappointed, and said that he would have to find quiet somewhere else. Then he asked whether there wasn't any house that would take him in as a boarder?"

She paused.

"Well?" I enquired.

"Oh, doctor, he seemed so strong and kind, and his eyes were so frank. I knew he was everything that a man ought to be. We were friends at once, and I hated the thought of losing him. It is not gay at Ravetot with only Jeanne to talk to from week's end to week's end. And then we are so poor—and you know we do take in paying guests when we can get them."

"I understand perfectly," said I.

She nodded. That was how it happened. Would a nice girl have done such a thing? I replied that if she knew as much of the ways of nice girls as I did, she would be astounded. She smiled wanly and went on with her artless story. Of course Mr. Everest jumped at the suggestion. It is not given to every young and un-lamenting widower to be housed beneath the same roof with so delicious a young woman as Pauline. He brought his luggage and took possession of the best spare room in the Villa, while Paul-ine and old, slatternly Jeanne, the *bonne à tout faire*, went about with agitated minds and busy hands attending to his comfort. Old Widdrington, however, in his morose chimney-corner, did not welcome the visitor. He growled and grumbled and rated his daughter for not having doubled the terms. Didn't she know they wanted every penny they could get? Something was wrong with his roulette machine which ought to be sent to Paris for repairs. Where was the money to come from? Pauline's father is the most unscrupulous, selfish old curmudgeon of my acquaint-ance!

Then, according to my young lady's incoherent and paren-thetic narrative, followed idyllic days. Pauline chattered to Mr. Everest in the morning, walked with him in the afternoon, pre-tended to play the piano to him in the evening, and in between times sat with him at meals. The inevitable happened. She had met no one like him before—he represented the strength and the music of the great world. He flashed upon her as the realisa-tion of the vague visions that had floated before her eyes when she stared seawards in the driving wind. That the man was a bit in love with her seems certain. I think that one day, when a wayside shed was sheltering them from the rain, he must have kissed her. A young girl's confidences are full of details; but the important ones are generally left out. They can be divined, however, by the old and experienced. At any rate, Pauline was radiantly happy, and Everest appeared contented to stay indefinitely at Ravetot and watch her happiness.

Thus far the story was ordinary enough. Given the circumstances it would have been extraordinary if my poor little Pauline had not fallen in love with the man and if the man's heart had not been touched. If he had found the girl's feelings too deep for his response and had precipitately bolted from a confused sense of acting honourably towards her, the story would also have been commonplace. The cause of his sudden riding away was peculiarly painful. Somehow I cannot blame him; and yet I am vain enough to imagine that I should have acted otherwise.

One morning Everest asked her if Jeanne might search his bedroom for a twenty-franc piece which he must have dropped on the floor. In the afternoon her father gave her twenty francs to get a postal order; he was sending to Paris for some fresh mechanism for his precious roulette-wheel. Everest accompanied her to the little Post Office. They walked arm in arm through the village like an affianced couple, and I fancy he must have said tenderer things than usual on the way, for at this stage of the story she wept. When she laid the louis on the stab below the *guichet*, she noticed that it was a a new Spanish coin. Spanish gold is rare. She showed it to Everest, and meeting his eyes read in them a curious questioning. The money order obtained, they continued their walk happily, and Pauline forgot the incident. Some days passed. Everest grew troubled and preoccupied. One live-long day he avoided her society altogether. She lived through it in a distressed wonder, and cried herself to sleep that night. How had she offended? The next morning he gravely announced his departure. Urgent affairs summoned him to Paris. In dazed misery she accepted the payment of his account and wrote him a receipt. His face was set like a mask, and he looked at her out of cold, stern eyes which frightened her. In a timid way she asked him if he were going without one kind word.

"There are times, Miss Widdrington," said he "when no word at all is the kindest."

"But what have I done?" she cried.

"Nothing at all but what is good and right. You may think whatever you like of me. Good-bye!"

He grasped his Gladstone bag, and through the window she saw him give it to the fisher-lad who was to carry it three miles to the nearest wayside station. He disappeared through the gate, and so out of her life. Fat, slatternly Jeanne came upon her a few moments later moaning her heart out, and administered comfort. It is very hard for Mademoiselle—but what could Mademoiselle expect? Monsieur Everest could not stay any longer in the house. Naturally. Of course, Monsieur was a little touched in the brain, with his eternal calculations—he was not responsible for his actions. Still, Monsieur Everest did not like Monsieur to take money out of his room. But, Great God of Pity! did not Mademoiselle know that was the reason of Monsieur Everest going away?

"It was father who had stolen the Spanish louis," cried Pauline in a passion of tears, as we leaned once more against the parapet of the jetty. "He also stole a fifty-franc note. Then he was caught red-handed by Mr. Everest rifling his despatch-box. Jeanne overheard them talking. It is horrible, horrible! How he must despise me! I feel wrapped in flames when I think of it— and I love him so—and I haven't slept for a week—and my heart is broken."

I could do little to soothe this paroxysm, save let it spend itself against my great-coat, while I again put my arm around her. The grey tide was leaping in and the fine spray dashed in my face. The early twilight began to settle over Ravetot, which appeared more desolate than ever.

"Never mind, my dear," said I, "you are young, and as your soul is sweet and clean you will get over this."

"Never," she moaned.

"You will leave Ravetot-sur-Mer and all its associations, and the brightness of life will drive all the shadows away."

"No. It is impossible. My heart is broken and I only want to stay here at the end of the jetty until I die."

"I shall die, anyhow," I remarked with a shiver, "if I stay here much longer, and I don't want to. Let us go home."

She assented. We walked away from the sea and struck the gloomy inland road. Then I said, somewhat meaningly:

"Haven't you the curiosity to enquire why I left my comfortable house in London to come to this God-forsaken hole?"

"Why did you, Doctor, dear?" she asked listlessly.

"To inform you that your cross old aunt Caroline is dead, that she has left you three thousand pounds a year under my trusteeship till you are five-and-twenty, and that I am going to carry off the rich and beautiful Miss Pauline Widdrington to England to-morrow."

She stood stock-still looking at me open-mouthed.

"Is it true?" she gasped.

"Of course," said I.

Her face was transfigured with a sudden radiance. Amazement, rapture, youth—the pulsating wonder of her twenty years danced in her eyes. In her excitement she pulled me by the lapels of my coat——

"*Doctor*! DOCTOR! Three thousand pounds a year! England! London! Men and women! Everything I've longed for! All the glad and beautiful things of life!"

"Yes, my dear."

She took my hands and swung them backwards and forwards.

"It's Heaven! Delicious Heaven!" she cried.

"But what about the broken heart?" I said maliciously.

She dropped my hands, sighed, and her face suddenly assumed an expression of portentous misery.

"I was forgetting. What does anything matter now? I shall never get over it. My heart *is* broken."

"Devil a bit, my dear," said I.

THE SCOURGE

I

Up to the death of his wife, that is to say for fifty-six years, Sir Hildebrand Oates held himself to be a very important and upright man, whose life not only was unassailable by slander, but even through the divine ordering of his being exempt from criticism. To the world and to himself he represented the incarnation of British impeccability, faultless from the little pink crown of his head to the tips of his toes correctly pedicured and unstained by purples of retributive gout. Except in church, where a conventional humility of attitude is imposed, his mind was blandly *conscia recti*. No ghost of sins committed disturbed his slumbers. He had committed no sin. He could tick off the Ten Commandments one by one with a serene conscience. He objected to profane swearing; he was a strict Sabbatarian; he had honoured his father and his mother and had erected a monument over their grave which added another fear of death to the beholder; he neither thieved nor murdered, nor followed in the footsteps of Don Juan, nor in those of his own infamous namesake; and being blessed in the world's goods, coveted nothing possessed by his neighbour—not even his wife, for his neighbours' wives could not compare in wifely meekness with his own. In thought, too, he had not sinned. Never, so far as he remembered, had he spoken a ribald word, never, indeed had he laughed at an unsavoury jest. It may be questioned whether he had laughed at any kind of joke whatsoever.

Sir Hildebrand stood for many things: for Public Morality; his name appeared on the committees of all the societies for the suppression of all the vices: for sound Liberalism and Incorruptible Government; he had poured much of his fortune into the party coffers and, to his astonishment, a gracious (and minister-harassed) Sovereign had conveyed recognition of his virtues in the form of a knighthood. For the sacred rights of the people; as Justice of the Peace he sentenced vagrants who slept in other people's barns to the severest penalties. For Principle in private life; in spite of the rending of his own heart and the agonized tears of his wife, he had cast off his undutiful children, a son and a daughter who had been guilty of the sin of disobedience and had run away taking their creaking destinies in their own hands. For the Sanctity of Home Life; night and morning he read prayers before the assembled household and dismissed any maidservant who committed the impropriety of conversing with a villager of the opposite sex. From youth up, his demeanour had been studiously grave and punctiliously courteous. A man of birth and breeding, he made it his ambition to be what he, with narrow definition, termed "a gentleman of the old school"; but being of Whig lineage, he had sat in Parliament as an hereditary Liberal and believed in Progressive Institutions.

It is difficult to give a flashlight picture of a human being at once so simple and so complex. An ardent Pharisee may serve as an epigrammatic characterisation. Hypocrite he was not. No miserable sinner more convinced of his rectitude, more devoid of pretence, ever walked the earth. Though his narrowness of view earned him but little love from his fellow-humans, his singleness of purpose, aided by an ample fortune, gained a measure of their respect. He lived irreproachable up to his standards. In an age of general scepticism he had unshakable faith. He believed intensely in himself. Now this passionate certitude of infallibility found, as far as his life's drama is concerned, its supreme expression in his relation to his wife, his children, and his money.

He married young. His wife brought him a fortune for which he was sole trustee, a couple of children, and a submissive obedience unparalleled in the most correct of Moslem house-holds. Eresby Manor, where they had lived for thirty years, was her own individual property, and she drew for pocket money some five hundred pounds a year. A timid, weak, sentimental soul, she was daunted from the first few frosty days of honey-moon by the inflexible personality of her husband. For thirty years she passed in the world's eye for little else than his shadow.

"My dear, you must allow me to judge in such matters," he would say in reply to mild remonstrance. And she deferred in-variably to his judgment. When his son Godfrey and his daugh-ter Sybil went their respective unfilial ways, it was enough for him to remark with cold eyes and slight, expressive gesture:

"My dear, distressing as I know it is to you, their conduct has broken my heart and I forbid the mention of their names in this house."

And the years passed and the perfect wife, though, in secret, she may have mourned like Rachel for her children, obeyed the very letter of her husband's law.

There remains the third vital point, to which I must refer, if I am to make comprehensible the strange story of Sir Hildebrand Oates. It was money—or, more explicitly, the diabolical caprice of finance—that first shook Sir Hildebrand's faith, not, perhaps, in his own infallibility, but in the harmonious co-operation of Divine Providence and himself. For the four or five years pre-ceding his wife's death his unerring instinct in financial affairs failed him. Speculations that promised indubitably the golden fruit of the Hesperides produced nothing but Dead Sea apples. He lost enormous sums of money. Irritability constricted both his brow and the old debonair "s" at the end of his signature. And when the County Guarantee Investment Society of which he was one of the original founders and directors called up unpaid balance on shares, and even then hovered on the verge of scan-dalous liquidation, Sir Hildebrand found himself racked with indignant anxiety.

He was sitting at a paper-strewn table in his library, a decorous library, a gentleman's library, lined from floor to ceiling with bookcases filled with books that no gentleman's library should be without, and trying to solve the eternal problem why two and two should not make forty, when the butler entered announcing the doctor.

"Ah, Thompson, glad to see you. What is it? Have you looked at Lady Oates? Been a bit queer for some days. These east winds. I hold them responsible for half the sickness of the county."

He threw up an accusing hand. If the east wind had been a human vagabond brought before Sir Hildebrand Oates, Justice of the Peace, it would have whined itself into a Zephyr. Sir Hildebrand's eyes looked blue and cold at offenders. From a stature of medium height he managed to extract the dignity of six-foot-two. Beneath a very long and very straight nose a grizzling moustache, dependent on the muscles of the thin lips as to whether it should go up or down, symbolised, as it were, the scales of justice. Sketches of accurately trimmed grey whiskers also indicated the exact balance of his mind. But to show that he was human and not impassionately divine, his thin hair once black, now greenish, was parted low down on the left side and brought straight over, leaving the little pink crown to which I have before alluded. His complexion was florid, disavowing atrabiliar prejudice. He had the long blunted chin of those secure of their destiny. He was extraordinarily clean.

The doctor said abruptly: "It's nothing to do with east winds. It's internal complications. I have to tell you she's very seriously ill."

A shadow of impatience passed over Sir Hildebrand's brow.

"Just like my wife," said he, "to fall ill, when I'm already half off my head with worry."

"The County Guarantee——?"

Sir Hildebrand nodded. The misfortunes of the Society were public property, and public too, within the fairly wide area of his acquaintance, was the knowledge of the fact that Sir Hildebrand was heavily involved therein. Too often had he vaunted the beneficent prosperity of the concern to which he had given his august support. At his own dinner-table men had dreaded the half-hour after the departure of the ladies, and at his club men had fled from him as they flee from the Baconian mythologist.

"It is a worry," the doctor admitted. "But financial preoccupations must give way"—he looked Sir Hildebrand clear in the eyes—"must give way before elementary questions of life and death."

"Death?" Sir Hildebrand regarded him blankly. How dare Death intrude in so unmannerly a fashion across his threshold?

"I should have been called in weeks ago," said the doctor. "All I can suggest now is that you should get Sir Almeric Home down from London. I'll telephone at once, with your authority. An operation may save her."

"By all means. But tell me—I had no idea—I wanted to send for you last week, but she's so obstinate—said it was mere indigestion."

"You should have sent for me all the same."

"Anyhow," said Sir Hildebrand, "tell me the worst."

The doctor told him and departed. Sir Hildebrand walked up and down his library, a man undeservedly stricken. The butler entered. Pringle, the chauffeur, desired audience.

Admitted, the man plunged into woeful apology. He had been trying the Mercédès on its return from an overhaul, and as he turned the corner by Rushworth Farm a motor lorry had run into him and smashed his head-lamps.

"I told you when I engaged you," said Sir Hildebrand, "that I allowed no accidents."

"It's only the lamps. I was driving most careful. The driver of the lorry owns himself in the wrong," pleaded the chauffeur.

"The merits or demerits of the case," replied Sir Hildebrand, "do not interest me. It's an accident. I don't allow accidents. You take a month's notice."

"Very well, Sir Hildebrand, but I do think it——"

"Enough," said Sir Hildebrand, dismissing him. "I have nothing more to hear from you or to say to you."

Then, when he was alone again, Sir Hildebrand reflected that noble resignation under misfortune was the part of a Christian gentleman, and in chastened mood went upstairs to see his wife. And in the days that followed, when Sir Almeric Home, summoned too late, had performed the useless wonders of his magical craft and had gone, Sir Hildebrand, most impeccable of husbands, visited the sick-room twice a day, making the most correct enquiries, beseeching her to name desires capable of fulfilment, and urbanely prophesying speedy return to health. At the end of the second visit he bent down and kissed her on the forehead. The ukase went forth to the servants' hall that no one should speak above a whisper, for fear of disturbing her ladyship, and the gardeners had orders to supply the sick-room with a daily profusion of flowers. Mortal gentleman could show no greater solicitude for a sick wife—save perhaps bring her a bunch of violets in his own hand. But with an automatic supply of orchids, why should he think of so trumpery an offering?

Lady Oates died. Sir Hildebrand accepted the stroke with Christian resignation. The Lord giveth and the Lord taketh away. Yet his house was desolate. He appreciated her virtues, which were many. He went categorically through her attributes: A faithful wife, a worthy mother of unworthy children, a capable manager, a submissive helpmate, a country gentlewoman of the old school who provided supremely for her husband's material comforts and never trespassed into the sphere of his intellectual and other masculine activities. His grief at the loss of his Eliza was sincere. The impending crash of the County Guarantee Investment Society ceased to trouble him. His own fortune had practically gone. Let it go. His dead wife's remained—sufficient to maintain his position in the county. As Dr. Thompson had rightly said, the vulgarities of finance must give way to the eternal sublimities of death. His wife, with whom he had lived for thirty years in a conjugal felicity unclouded save by the unforgivable sins of his children now exiled through their own wilfulness to remote parts of the Empire, was dead. The stupendous fact eclipsed all other facts in a fact-riveted universe. Lady Oates who, after the way of women of limited outlook, had always taken a great interest in funerals, had the funeral of her life. The Bishop of the Diocese conducted the funeral service. The County, headed by the old Duke of Dunster, his neighbour, followed her to the grave.

II

"She was a good Christian woman, Haversham," said Sir Hildebrand later in the day. "I did not deserve her. But I think I may feel that I did my best all my life to ensure her happiness."

"No doubt, of course," replied Haversham, the county lawyer. "Er—don't you think we might get this formal business over? I've brought Lady Oates's will in my pocket."

He drew out a sealed envelope. Sir Hildebrand held out his hand. The lawyer shook his head. "I'm executor—it's written on the outside—I must open it."

"You executor? That's rather strange," said Sir Hildebrand.

Haversham opened the envelope, adjusted his glasses, and glanced through the document. Then he took off his glasses and his brows wrinkled, and with a queer look, half scared, half malicious, in his eyes, gazed at Sir Hildebrand.

"I must tell you, my dear Oates," said he, after a moment or so, "that I had nothing to do with the making of this. Nothing whatsoever. Lady Oates called at my office about two years ago and placed the sealed envelope in my charge. I had no idea of the contents till this minute."

"Let me see," said Sir Hildebrand; and again he stretched out his hand.

Haversham, holding the paper, hesitated for a few seconds. "I'm afraid I must read it to you, there being no third party present."

"Third party? What do you mean?"

"A witness. A formal precaution." The lawyer again put on his glasses. "The introductory matter is the ordinary phraseology of the printed form one buys at stationers' shops—naming me executor." Then he read aloud:

"I will and bequeath to my husband, Sir Hildebrand Oates, Knight, the sum of fifteen shillings to buy himself a scourge to do penance for the arrogance, uncharitableness and cruelty with which he has treated myself and my beloved children for the last thirty years. I bequeath to my son Godfrey the house and estate of Eresby Manor and all the furniture, plate, jewels, livestock and everything of mine comprised therein. The residue of my possessions I bequeath to my son Godfrey and my daughter Sybil, in equal shares. I leave it to my children to act generously by my old servants, and my horses and dogs."

Sir Hildebrand's florid face grew purple. He looked fishy-eyed and open-mouthed at the lawyer, and gurgled horribly in his throat. Haversham hastily rang a bell. The butler appeared. Between them they carried Sir Hildebrand up to bed and sent for the doctor.

III

When Sir Hildebrand recovered, which he did quickly, he went about like a man in a daze, stupefied by his wife's hideous accusation and monstrous ingratitude. It was inconceivable that the submissive angel with whom he had lived and the secret writer of those appalling words should be one and the same person. Surely, insanity. That invalidated the will. But Haversham pointed out that insanity would have to be proved, which was impossible. The will contained no legal flaw. Lady Oates's dispositions would have to be carried out.

"It leaves me practically a pauper," said Sir Hildebrand, whereat the other, imperceptibly, shrugged his shoulders.

He realised, in cold terror, that the house wherein he dwelt was his no longer. Even the chairs and tables belonged to his son, Godfrey. His own personal belongings could be carried away in a couple of handcarts. Instead of thousands his income had suddenly dwindled to a salvage of a few hundreds a year. From his position in the county he had tumbled with the suddenness and irreparability of Humpty-Dumpty! All the vanities of his life sprang on him and choked him. He was a person of no importance whatever. He gasped. Had mere outside misfortune beset him, he doubtless would have faced his downfall with the courage of a gentleman of the old school. His soul would have been untouched. But now it was stabbed, and with an envenomed blade. His wife had brought him to bitter shame.... "Arrogance, uncharitableness, cruelty." The denunciation rang in his head day and night. He arrogant, uncharitable, cruel? The charge staggered reason. His indignant glance sweeping backward through the years could see nothing in his life but continuous humility, charity, and kindness. He had not deviated a hair's breath from irreproachable standards of conduct. Arrogant? When Sybil, engaged in consequences of his tender sagacity to a neighbouring magnate, a widowed ironmaster, eloped, at dead of night on her wedding eve, with a penniless subaltern in the Indian Army, he suffered humiliation before the countryside, with manly dignity. No less humiliating had been his position and no less resigned his attitude when Godfrey, declining to obey the tee-total, non-smoking, early-to-bed, early-to-breakfast rules of the house, declining also to be ordained and take up the living of Thereon in the gift of the Lady of the Manor of Eresby, went off, in undutiful passion, to Canada to pursue some godless and precarious career. Uncharitableness? Cruelty? His children had defied him, and with callous barbarity had cut all filial ties. And his wife? She had lived in cotton-wool all her days. It was she who had been cruel—inconceivably malignant.

IV

Sir Hildebrand, after giving Haversham, the lawyer, an account of his stewardship—in his wild investments he had not imperilled a penny of his wife's money—resigned his county appointments, chairmanships and presidentships and memberships of committees, went to London and took a room at his club. Rumour of his fallen fortunes spread quickly. He found himself neither shunned nor snubbed, but not welcomed in the inner smoke-room coterie before which, as a wealthy and important county gentleman, he had been wont to lay down the law. No longer was he Sir Oracle. Sensitive to the subtle changes he attributed them to the rank snobbery of his fellow-members. No doubt he was right. The delicate point of snobbery that he did not realise was the difference between the degrees of sufferance accorded to the rich bore and the poor bore. In the eyes of the club, Sir Hildebrand Oates was the poor bore. He became freezingly aware of a devastating loneliness. In the meanwhile his children had written the correctest of letters. Deep grief for mother's death was the keynote of each. With regard to worldly matters, Sybil confessed that the legacy made a revolution in her plans for her children's future, but would not affect her present movements, as she could not allow her husband to abandon a career which promised to be brilliant. She would be home in a couple of years. The son, Godfrey, welcomed the unexpected fortune. The small business he had got together just needed this capital to expand into gigantic proportions. It would be two or three years before he could leave it. In the meantime, he hoped his father would not dream of leaving Eresby Manor. Neither son nor daughter seemed to be aware of Sir Hildebrand's impoverishment. Also, neither of them expressed sympathy for, or even alluded to, the grief that he himself must be suffering. The omission puzzled him; for he had the lawyer's assurance that they should remain ignorant, as far as lay in his power, of the dreadful text of the will. Did the omission arise from doubt in their minds as to his love for their mother and the genuineness of his sorrow at her death? To solve the riddle, Sir Hildebrand began to think as he had never thought before.

V

Arrogance, uncharitableness, and cruelty. To wife and children. For thirty years. Fifteen shillings to buy a scourge wherewith to do penance. He could think of nothing else by day or night. The earth beneath his feet which he had deemed so solid became a quagmire, so that he knew not where to step. And the serene air darkened. The roots of his being suffered cataclysm. Either his wife had been some mad monster in human form, or her terrible indictment had some basis of truth. The man's soul writhed in the flame of the blazing words. A scourge for penance. Fifteen shillings to buy it with. In due course he received the ghastly cheque from Haversham. His first impulse was to tear it to pieces; his second, to fold it up and put it in his letter-case. At the end of a business meeting with Haversham a day or two later, he asked him point-blank:

"Why did you insult me by sending me the cheque for fifteen shillings?"

"It was a legal formality with which I was bound to comply."

"De minimis non curet lex," said Sir Hildebrand. "No one pays barley-corn rent or farthing damages or the shilling consideration in a contract. Your action implies malicious agreement with Lady Oates' opinion of me."

He bent his head forward and looked at Haversham with feverish intensity. Haversham had old scores to settle. The importance, omniscience, perfection, and condescending urbanity of Sir Hildebrand had rasped his nerves for a quarter of a century. If there was one living man whom he hated wholeheartedly, and over whose humiliation he rejoiced, it was Sir Hildebrand Oates. He yielded to the swift temptation. He rose hastily and gathered up his papers.

"If you can find me a human creature in this universe who doesn't share Lady Oates's opinion, I will give him every penny I am worth."

He went out, and then overcome with remorse for having kicked a fallen man, felt inclined to hang himself. But he knew that he had spoken truly. Meanwhile Sir Hildebrand walked up and down the little visitors' room at the club, where the interview had taken place, passing his hand over his indeterminate moustache and long blunt chin. He felt neither anger nor indignation—but rather the dazed dismay of a prisoner to whom the judge deals a severer sentence than he expected. After a while he sat at a small table and prepared to write a letter connected with the business matters he had just discussed with Haversham. But the words would not come, his brain was fogged; he went off into a reverie, and awoke to find himself scribbling in arabesque, "Fifteen shillings to buy a scourge."

After a solitary dinner at the club that evening he discovered in a remote corner of the smoking-room, a life-long acquaintance, an old schoolfellow, one Colonel Bagot, reading a newspaper. He approached.

"Good evening, Bagot."

Colonel Bagot raised his eyes from the paper, nodded, and resumed his reading. Sir Hildebrand deliberately wheeled a chair to his side and sat down.

"Can I have a word or two with you?"

"Certainly, my dear fellow," Bagot replied, putting down his paper.

"What kind of a boy was I at school?"

"What kind of a ... what the deuce do you mean?" asked the astonished colonel.

"I want you to tell me what kind of a boy I was," said Sir Hildebrand gravely.

"Just an ordinary chap."

"Would you have called me modest, generous, and kind?"

"What in God's name are you driving at?" asked the Colonel, twisting himself round on his chair.

"At your opinion of me. Was I modest, generous, and kind? It's a vital question."

"It's a damned embarrassing one to put to a man during the process of digestion. Well, you know, Oates, you always were a queer beggar. If I had had the summing up of you I should have said: 'Free from vice.'"

"Negative."

"Well, yes—in a way—but——"

"You've answered me. Now another. Do you think I treated my children badly?"

"Really, Oates—oh, confound it!" Angrily he dusted himself free from the long ash that had fallen from his cigar. "I don't see why I should be asked such a question."

"I do. You've known me all your life. I want you to answer it frankly."

Colonel Bagot was stout, red, and choleric. Sir Hildebrand irritated him. If he was looking for trouble, he should have it. "I think you treated them abominably—there!" said he.

"Thank you," said Sir Hildebrand.

"What?" gasped Bagot.

"I said 'thank you.' And lastly—you have had many opportunities of judging—do you think I did all in my power to make my wife happy?"

At first Bagot made a gesture of impatience. His position was both grotesque and intolerable. Was Oates going mad? Answering the surmise, Sir Hildebrand said:

"I'm aware my question is extraordinary, perhaps outrageous; but I am quite sane. Did she look crushed, down-trodden, as though she were not allowed to have a will of her own?"

It was impossible not to see that the man was in a dry agony of earnestness. Irritation and annoyance fell like garments from Bagot's shoulders.

"You really want to get at the exact truth, as far as I can give it you?"

"From the depth of my soul," said Sir Hildebrand.

"Then," answered Bagot, quite simply, "I'm sorry to say unpleasant things. But I think Lady Oates led a dog's life—and so does everybody."

"That's just what I wanted to be sure of," said Sir Hildebrand, rising. He bent his head courteously. "Good night, Bagot," and he went away with dreary dignity.

VI

A cloud settled on Sir Hildebrand's mind through which he saw immediate things murkily. He passed days of unaccustomed loneliness and inaction. He walked the familiar streets of London like one in a dream. One afternoon he found himself gazing with unspeculative eye into the window of a small Roman Catholic Repository where crucifixes and statues of the Virgin and Child and rosaries and religious books and pictures were exposed for sale. Until realisation of the objects at which he had been staring dawned upon his mind, he had not been aware of the nature of the shop. The shadow of a smile passed over his face. He entered. An old man with a long white beard was behind the counter.

"Do you keep scourges?" asked Sir Hildebrand.

"No, sir," replied the old man, somewhat astonished.

"That's unfortunate—very unfortunate," said Sir Hildebrand, regarding him dully. "I'm in need of one."

"Even among certain of the religious orders the Discipline is forbidden nowadays," replied the old man.

"Among certain others it is practised?"

"I believe so."

"Then scourges are procurable. I will ask you to get one—or have one made according to religious pattern. I will pay fifteen shillings for it."

"It could not possibly cost that—a mere matter of wood and

string."

"I will pay neither more nor less," said Sir Hildebrand, laying on the counter the cheque which he had endorsed and his card. "I—I have made a vow. It's a matter of conscience. Kindly send it to the club address."

He walked out of the shop somewhat lighter of heart, his instinct for the scrupulous satisfied. The abominable cheque no longer burned through letter-case and raiment and body and corroded his soul. He had devoted the money to the purpose for which it was ear-marked. The precision was soothed. In puzzling darkness he had also taken an enormous psychological stride.

The familiar club became unbearable, his fellow-members abhorrent. Friends and acquaintances outside—and they were legion—who, taking pity on his loneliness, sought him out and invited him to their houses, he shunned in a curious terror. He was forever meeting them in the streets. Behind their masks of sympathy he read his wife's deadly accusation and its confirmation which he had received from Haversham and Bagot. When the scourge arrived—a business-like instrument in a cardboard box—he sat for a long time in his club bedroom drawing the knotted cords between his fingers, lost in retrospective thought…. And suddenly a scene flashed across his mind. Venice. The first days of their honeymoon. The sun-baked Renaissance façade of a church in a Campo bounded by a canal where their gondola lay waiting. A tattered, one-legged, be-crutched beggar holding out his hat by the church door…. He, Hildebrand, stalked majestically past, his wife following. Near the *fondamenta* he turned and discovered her in the act of tendering from her purse a two-lire piece to the beggar who had hobbled expectant in her wake. Hildebrand interposed a hand; the shock accidentally jerked the coin from hers. It rolled. The one-legged beggar threw himself prone, in order to seize it. But it rolled into the canal. An agony of despair and supplication mounted from the tatterdemalion's eyes.

"Oh, Hildebrand, give him another."

"Certainly not," he replied. "It's immoral to encourage mendicity."

She wept in the gondola. He thought her silly, and told her so. They landed at the Molo and he took her to drink chocolate at Florian's on the Piazza. She bent her meek head over the cup and the tears fell into it. A well-dressed Venetian couple who sat at the next table stared at her, passed remarks, and giggled outright with the ordinary and exquisite Italian politeness.

"My dear Eliza," said Hildebrand, "if you can't help being a victim to sickly sentimentality, at least, as my wife, you must learn to control yourself in public."

And meekly she controlled herself and drank her salted chocolate. In compliance with a timidly expressed desire, and in order to show his forgiveness, he escorted her into the open square, and like any vulgar Cook's tourist bought her a paper cornet of dried peas, wherewith, to his self-conscious martyrdom, she fed the pigeons. Seeing an old man some way off do the same, she scattered a few grains along the curled-up brim of her Leghorn hat; and presently, so still she was and gracious, an iridescent swarm enveloped her, eating from both hands outstretched and encircling her head like a halo. For the moment she was the embodiment of innocent happiness. But Hildebrand thought her notoriously absurd, and when he saw Lord and Lady Benham approaching them from the Piazzetta, he stepped forward and with an abrupt gesture sent the pigeons scurrying away. And she looked for the vanished birds with much the same scared piteousness as the one-legged beggar had looked for the lost two-lire piece.

After thirty years the memory of that afternoon flamed vivid, as he drew the strings of the idle scourge between his fingers. And then the puzzling darkness overspread his mind.

After a while he replaced the scourge in the cardboard box and summoned the club valet.

"Pack up all my things," said he. "I am going abroad to-morrow by the eleven o'clock train from Victoria."

VII

Few English-speaking and, stranger still, few German-speaking guests stay at the Albergo Tonelli in Venice. For one thing, it has not many rooms; for another, it is far from the Grand Canal; and for yet another, the fat proprietor Ettore Tonelli and his fatter wife are too sluggish of body and brain to worry about *forestieri* who have to be communicated with in outlandish tongues, and, for their supposed comfort, demand all sorts of exotic foolishness such as baths, punctuality, and information as to the whereabouts of fusty old pictures and the exact tariff of gondolas. The house was filled from year's end to year's end with Italian commercial travellers; and Ettore's ways and their ways corresponded to a nicety. The Albergo Tonelli was a little red-brick fifteenth-century palazzo, its Lombardic crocketed windows gaily picked out in white, and it dominated the *campiello* wherein it was situated. In the centre of the tiny square was a marble well-head richly carved, and by its side a pump from which the inhabitants of the vague tumble-down circumambient dwellings drew the water to wash the underlinen which hung to dry from the windows. A great segment of the corner diagonally opposite the Albergo was occupied by the bare and rudely swelling brick apse of a seventeenth-century church. Two inconsiderable thoroughfares, *calle* five foot wide, lead from the *campiello* to the wide world of Venice.

It was hither that Sir Hildebrand Oates, after a week of nerve-shattering tumult at one of the great Grand Canal hotels, and after horrified examination of the question of balance of expenditure over income, found his way through the kind offices of a gondolier to whom he had promised twenty francs if he could conduct him to the forgotten church, the memorable scene of the adventure of the beggar and the two-franc piece. With unerring instinct the gondolier had rowed him to Santa Maria Formosa, the very spot. Sir Hildebrand troubled himself neither with the church nor the heart-easing wonder of Palma Vecchio's Santa Barbara within, but, with bent brow, traced the course of the lame beggar from the step to the *fondamenta*, and the course of the rolling coin from his Eliza's hand into the canal. Then he paused for a few moments deep in thought, and finally drew a two-lire piece from his pocket, and, recrossing the Campo, handed it gravely to a beggar-woman, the successor of the lame man, who sat sunning herself on the spacious marble seat by the side of the great door. When he returned to the hotel he gave the gondolier his colossal reward and made a friend for life. Giuseppe delighted at finding an English gentleman who could converse readily hi Italian—for Sir Hildebrand, a man of considerable culture, possessed a working knowledge of three or four European languages—expressed his gratitude on subsequent excursions, by overflowing with picturesque anecdote, both historical and personal. A pathetic craving for intercourse with his kind and the solace of obtaining it from one remote from his social environment drew Sir Hildebrand into queer sympathy with a genuine human being. Giuseppe treated him with a respectful familiarity which he had never before encountered in a member of the lower classes. One afternoon, on the silent *lagune* side of the Giudecca, turning round on his cushions, he confided to the lean, bronzed, rhythmically working figure standing behind him, something of the puzzledom of his soul. Guiseppe, in the practical Italian way, interpreted the confidences as a desire to escape from the tourist-agitated and fantastically expensive quarters of the city into some unruffled haven. That evening he interviewed the second cousin of his wife, the Signora Tonelli of the Albergo of that name, and the next day Sir Hildebrand took possession of the front room overlooking the *campiello*, on the *piano nobile* or second floor of the hotel.

And here Sir Hildebrand Oates, Knight, once Member of Parliament, Lord of the Manor, Chairman of Quarter Sessions, Director of great companies, orchid rival of His Grace the Duke of Dunster, important and impeccable personage, the exact temperature of whose bath water had been to a trembling household a matter of as much vital concern as the salvation of their own souls—entered upon a life of queer discomfort, privation and humility. For the first time in his life he experienced the hugger-mugger makeshift of the bed-sitting room—a chamber, too, cold and comfortless, with one scraggy rug by the bedside to mitigate the rigour of an inlaid floor looking like a galantine of veal, once the pride of the palazzo, and meagrely furnished with the barest objects of necessity, and these of monstrous and incongruous ugliness; and he learned in the redolent restaurant downstairs, the way to eat spaghetti like a contented beast and the relish of sour wine and the overrated importance of the cleanliness of cutlery. In his dignified acceptance of surroundings that to him were squalid, he manifested his essential breeding. The correct courtesy of his demeanour gained for the *illustrissimo signore inglese* the wholehearted respect of the Signore and Signora Tonelli. And the famous scourge nailed (symbolically) over his hard little bed procured him a terrible reputation for piety in the *parrocchia*. After a while, indeed, as soon as he had settled to his new mode of living, the inveterate habit of punctilio caused him, almost unconsciously, to fix by the clock his day's routine. Called at eight o'clock, a kind of eight conjectured by the good-humoured, tousled sloven of a chambermaid, he dressed with scrupulous care. At nine he descended for his morning coffee to the chill deserted restaurant—for all the revolution in his existence he could not commit the immorality of breakfasting in his bedroom. At half-past he regained his room, where, till eleven, he wrote by the window overlooking the urchin-resonant *campiello*. Then with gloves and cane, to outward appearance the immaculate, the impeccable Sir Hildebrand Oates of Eresby Manor, he walked through the narrow, twisting streets and over bridges and across *campi* and *campiello* to the Piazza San Marco. As soon as he neared the east-end of the great square, a seller of corn and peas approached him, handed him a paper cornet, from which Sir Hildebrand, with awful gravity, fed the pigeons. And the pigeons looked for him, too; and they perched on his arms and his shoulders and even on the crown of his Homburg hat, the brim of which he had, by way of solemn rite, filled with grain, until the gaunt, grey, unsmiling man was hidden in fluttering iridescence. And tourists and idlers used to come every day and look at him, as at one of the sights of Venice. The supply finished, Sir Hildebrand went to the Café Florian on the south of the Piazza and ordering a *sirop* which he seldom drank, read the *Corriere de la Sera*, until the midday gun sent the pigeons whirring to their favourite cornices. Then Sir Hildebrand retraced his steps to the Albergo Tonelli, lunched, read till three, wrote till five, and again went out to take the air. Dinner, half an hour's courtly gossip in the cramped and smelly apology for a lounge, with landlord or a commercial traveller disinclined for theatre or music-hall, or the absorbing amusement of Venice, walking in the Piazza or along the Riva Schiavoni, and then to read or write till bedtime.

No Englishman of any social position can stand daily in the Piazza San Marco without now and then coming across acquaintances, least of all a man of such importance in his day as Sir Hildebrand Oates. He accepted the greetings of chance-met friends with courteous resignation.

"We're at the Hôtel de l'Europe. Where are you staying, Sir Hildebrand?"

"I live in Venice, I have made it my home. You see the birds accept me as one of themselves."

"You'll come and dine with us, won't you?"

"I should love to," Sir Hildebrand would reply; "but for the next month or so I am overwhelmed with work. I'm so sorry. If you have any time to spare, and would like to get off the beaten track, let me recommend you to wander through the Giudecca on foot. I hope Lady Elizabeth is well. I'm so glad. Will you give her my kindest regards? Good-bye." And Sir Hildebrand would make his irreproachable bow and take his leave. No one learned where he had made his home in Venice. In fact, no one but Messrs. Thomas Cook and Son knew his address. He banked with them and they forwarded his letters to the Albergo Tonelli.

It has been said that Sir Hildebrand occupied much of his time in writing, and he himself declared that he was overwhelmed with work. He was indeed engaged in an absorbing task of literary composition, and his reference library consisted in thirty or forty leather-covered volumes each fitted with a clasp and lock, of which the key hung at the end of his watchchain; and every page of every volume was filled with his own small, precise handwriting. He made slow progress, for the work demanded concentrated thought and close reasoning. The rumour of his occupation having spread through the parrocchia, he acquired, in addition to that of a pietist, the reputation of an *erudito*. He became the pride of the *campiello*. When he crossed the little square, the inhabitants pointed him out to less fortunate out-dwellers. There was the great English noble who had made vows of poverty, and gave himself the Discipline and wrote wonderful works of Theology. And men touched their hats and women saluted shyly, and Sir Hildebrand punctiliously, and with a queer pathetic gratitude, responded. Even the children gave him a "Buon giorno, Signore," and smiled up into his face, unconscious of the pious scholar he was supposed to be, and of the almighty potentate that he had been. Once, yielding to an obscure though powerful instinct, he purchased in the Merceria a packet of chocolates, and on entering his *campiello* presented them, with stupendous gravity concealing extreme embarrassment, to a little gang of urchins. Encouraged by a dazzling success, he made it a rule to distribute sweetmeats every Saturday morning to the children of the *campiello*. After a while he learned their names and idiosyncrasies, and held solemn though kindly speech with them, manifesting an interest in their games and questioning them sympathetically as to their scholastic attainments. Sometimes gathering from their talk a notion of the desperate poverty of parents, he put a lire or two into grubby little fists, in spite of a lifelong conviction of the immorality of indiscriminate almsgiving; and dark, haggard mothers blessed him, and stood in his way to catch his smile. All of which was pleasant, though exceedingly puzzling to Sir Hildebrand Oates.

VIII

Between two and three years after their mother's death, Sir Hildebrand's son and daughter, who bore each other a devoted affection and carried on a constant correspondence, arranged to meet in England, Godfrey travelling from Canada, Sybil, with her children, from India. The first thing they learned (from Haversham, the lawyer) was the extent of their father's financial ruin. They knew—many kind friends had told them—that he had had losses and had retired from public life; but, living out of the world, and accepting their childhood's tradition of his incalculable wealth, they had taken it for granted that he continued to lead a life of elegant luxury. When Haversham, one of the few people who really knew, informed them (with a revengeful smile) that their father could not possibly have more than a hundred or two a year, they were shocked to the depths of their clean, matter-of-fact English souls. The Great Panjandrum, arbiter of destinies, had been brought low, was living in obscurity in Italy. The pity of it! As they interchanged glances the same thought leaped into the eyes of each.

"We must look him up and see what can be done," said Godfrey.

"Of course, dear," said Sybil.

"I offered him the use of Eresby, but he was too proud to take it."

"And I never offered him anything at all," said Sybil.

"I should advise you," said Haversham, "to leave Sir Hildebrand alone."

Godfrey, a high-mettled young man and one who was accustomed to arrive at his own decisions, and moreover did not like Haversham, gripped his sister by the arm.

"Whatever advice you give me, Mr. Haversham, I will take just when I think it necessary."

"That is the attitude of most of my clients," replied Haversham dryly, "whether it is a sound attitude or not——" he waved an expressive hand.

"We'll go and hunt him up, anyway," said Godfrey. "If he's impossible, we can come back. If he isn't—so much the better. What do you say, Sybil?"

Sybil said what he knew she would say.

"Sir Hildebrand's address is vague," remarked Haversham. "Cook's, Venice."

"What more, in Hades, do we want?" cried the young man.

So, after Sybil had made arrangements for the safe keeping of her offspring, and Godfrey and herself had written to announce their coming, the pair set out for Venice.

"We are very sorry, but we are unable to give you Sir Hildebrand Oates's address," said Messrs. Thomas Cook and Son.

Godfrey protested. "We are his son and daughter," he said, in effect. "We have reason to believe our father is living in poverty. We have written and he has not replied. We must find him."

Identity established, Messrs. Thomas Cook and Son disclosed the whereabouts of their customer. A gondola took brother and sister to the *Campo* facing the west front of the church behind which lay the *Campiello* where the hotel was situated. Their hearts sank low as they beheld the mildewed decay of the Albergo Tonelli, lower as they entered the cool, canal-smelling *trattoria*—or restaurant, the main entrance to the Albergo. Signore Tonelli in shirt sleeves greeted them. What was their pleasure?

"Sir Hildebrand Oates?"

At first from his rapid and incomprehensible Italian they could gather little else than the fact of their father's absence from home. After a while the reiteration of the words *ospedale inglese* made an impression on their minds.

"*Malade?*" asked Sybil, trying the only foreign language with which she had a slight acquaintance.

"*Si, si!*" cried Tonelli, delighted at eventual understanding.

And then a Providence-sent bagman who spoke a little English came out and interpreted.

The *illustrissimo signore* was ill. A pneumonia. He had stood to feed the pigeons in the rain, in the northeast wind, and had contracted a chill. When they thought he was dying, they sent for the English doctor who had attended him before for trifling ailments, and unconscious he had been transported to the English hospital in the Giudecca. And there he was now. A thousand pities he should die. The dearest and most revered man. The whole neighbourhood who loved him was stricken with grief. They prayed for him in the church, the signore and signora could see it there, and vows and candles had been made to the Virgin, the Blessed Mother, for he too loved all children. Signore Tonelli, joined by this time by his wife, exaggerated perhaps in the imaginative Italian way. But every tone and gesture sprang from deep sincerity. Brother and sister looked at each other in dumb wonder.

"*Ecco, Elizabetta!*" Tonelli, commanding the doorway of the restaurant, summoned an elderly woman from the pump by the well-head and discoursed volubly. She approached the young English couple and also volubly discoursed. The interpreter interpreted. They gained confirmation of the amazing fact that, in this squalid, stone-flagged, rickety little square, Sir Hildebrand had managed to make himself beloved. Childhood's memories rose within them, half-caught, but haunting sayings of servants and villagers which had impressed upon their minds the detestation in which he was held in their Somersetshire home.

Godfrey turned to his sister. "Well, I'm damned," said he.

"I should like to see his rooms," said Sybil.

The interpreter again interpreted. The Tonellis threw out their arms. Of course they could visit the apartment of the *illustrissimo signore*. They were led upstairs and ushered into the chill, dark bed-sitting-room, as ascetic as a monk's cell, and both gasped when they beheld the flagellum hanging from its nail over the bed. They requested privacy. The Tonellis and the bagman-interpreter retired.

"What the devil's the meaning of it?" said Godfrey.

Sybil, kind-hearted, began to cry. Something strange and piteous, something elusive had happened. The awful, poverty-stricken room chilled her blood, and the sight of the venomous scourge froze it. She caught and held Godfrey's hand. Had their father gone over to Rome and turned ascetic? They looked bewildered around the room. But no other sign, crucifix, rosary, sacred picture, betokened the pious convert. They scanned the rough deal bookshelf. A few dull volumes of English classics, a few works on sociology in French and Italian, a flagrantly staring red *Burke's Landed Gentry*, and that was practically all the library. Not one book of devotion was visible, save the Bible, the Book of Common Prayer, and a little vellum-covered Elzevir edition of Saint Augustine's *Flammulæ Amoris*, which Godfrey remembered from childhood on account of its quaint woodcuts. They could see nothing indicative of religious life but the flagellum over the bed—and that seemed curiously new and unused. Again they looked around the bare characterless room, characteristic only of its occupant by its scrupulous tidiness;

yet one object at last attracted their attention. On a deal writing-table by the window lay a thick pile of manuscript. Godfrey turned the brown paper covering. Standing together, brother and sister read the astounding title-page:

"An enquiry into my wife's justification for the following terms of her will:—

"'I will and bequeath to my husband, Sir Hildebrand Oates, Knight, the sum of fifteen shillings to buy himself a scourge to do penance for the arrogance, uncharitableness and cruelty with which he has treated myself and my beloved children for the last thirty years.'

"This dispassionate enquiry I dedicate to my son Godfrey and my daughter Sybil."

Brother and sister regarded each other with drawn faces and mutually questioning eyes.

"We can't leave this lying about," said Godfrey. And he tucked the manuscript under his arm.

The gondola took them through the narrow waterways to the Grand Canal of the Giudecca, where, on the Zattere side, all the wave-worn merchant shipping of Venice and Trieste and Fiume and Genoa finds momentary rest, and across to the low bridge-archway of the canal cutting through the island, on the side of which is Lady Layard's modest English hospital. Yes, said the matron, Sir Hildebrand was there. Pneumonia. Getting on as well as could be expected; but impossible to see him. She would telephone to their hotel in the morning.

That night, until dawn, Godfrey read the manuscript, a document of soul-gripping interest. It was neither an *apologia pro vita sua*, nor a breast-beating *peccavi* cry of confession; but a minute analysis of every remembered incident in the relations between his family and himself from the first pragmatical days of his wedding journey. And judicially he delivered judgments in the terse, lucid French form. "Whereas I, etc., etc...." and "whereas my wife, etc., etc...."—setting forth and balancing the facts—"it is my opinion that I acted arrogantly," or "uncharitably," or "cruelly." Now and again, though rarely, the judgments went in his favour. But invariably the words were added: "I am willing, however, in this case, to submit to the decision of any arbitrator or court of appeal my children may think it worthwhile to appoint."

The last words, scrawled shakily in pencil, were:

"I have not, to my great regret, been able to bring this record up-to-date; but as I am very ill and, at my age, may not recover, I feel it my duty to say that, as far as my two years' painful examination into my past life warrants my judgment, I am of the opinion that my wife had ample justification for the terms she employed regarding me in her will. Furthermore, if, as is probable, I should die of my illness, I should like my children to know that long ere this I have deeply desired in my loneliness to stretch out my arms to them in affection and beg their forgiveness, but that I have been prevented from so doing by the appalling fear that, I being now very poor and they being very rich, my overtures, considering the lack of affection I have exhibited to them in the past might be misinterpreted. The British Consul here, who has kindly consented to be my executor, will..."

And then strength had evidently failed him and he could write no more.

The next morning Godfrey related to his sister what he had read and gave her the manuscript to read at her convenience; and together they went to the hospital and obtained from the doctor his somewhat pessimistic report; and then again they visited the Albergo Tonelli and learned more of the strange, stiff and benevolent life of Sir Hildebrand Oates. Once more they mounted to the cold cheerless room where their father had spent the past two years. Godfrey unhooked the scourge from the nail.

"What are you going to do?" Sybil asked, her eyes full of tears.

"I'm going to burn the damned thing. Whether he lives or dies, the poor old chap's penance is at an end. By God! he has done enough." He turned upon her swiftly. "You don't feel any resentment against him now, do you?"

"Resentment?" Her voice broke on the word and she cast herself on the hard little bed and sobbed.

IX

And so it came to pass that a new Sir Hildebrand Oates, with a humble and a contrite heart, which we are told the Lord doth not despise, came into residence once more at Eresby Manor, agent for his son and guardian of his daughter's children. Godfrey transferred his legal business from Haversham to a younger practitioner in the neighbourhood to whom Sir Hildebrand showed a stately deference. And every day, being a man of habit —instinctive habit which no revolution of the soul can alter —he visited his wife's grave in the little churchyard, a stone's throw from the manor house, and in his fancy a cloud of pigeons came iridescent, darkening the air....

The County called, but he held himself aloof. He was no longer the all-important unassailable man. He had come through many fires to a wisdom undreamed of by the County. Human love had touched him with its simple angel wing— the love of son and daughter, the love of the rude souls in the squalid Venetian *Campiello*; and the patter of children's feet, the soft and trusting touch of children's hands, the glad welcome of children's voices, had brought him back to the elemental wells of happiness.

One afternoon, the butler entering the dining-room with the announcement "His Grace, the Duke of——" gasped, unable to finish the title. For there was Sir Hildebrand Oates—younger at fifty-nine than he was at thirty—lying prone on the hearth-rug, with a pair of flushed infants astride on the softer portions of his back, using the once almighty man as a being of little account. Sir Hildebrand turned his long chin and long nose up towards his visitor, and there was a new smile in his eyes.

"Sorry, Duke," said he, "but you see, I can't get up."

MY SHADOW FRIENDS

My gentle readers have been good enough to ask me what some of the folk whose adventures I have from time to time described have done in the Great War. It is a large question, for they are so many. Most of them have done things they never dreamed they would be called upon to do. Those that survived till 1914 have worked, like the rest of the community in England and France, according to their several capacities, in the Holiest Crusade in the history of mankind.

Well, let me plunge at once into the midst of things.

About a year ago the great voice of Jaffery came booming across my lawn. He was a Lieutenant-Colonel, and a D.S.O., and his great red beard had gone. The same, but yet a subtly different Jaffery. Liosha was driving a motor-lorry in France. He told me she was having the time of her life.

I have heard, too, of my old friend Sir Marcus, leaner than ever and clad in ill-fitting khaki, and sitting in a dreary office in Havre with piles of browny-yellow army forms before him, on which he had checked packing-cases of bully-beef ever since the war began. And if you visit a certain hospital—in Manchester of all places, so dislocating has been the war—there you will still see Lady Ordeyne (it always gives me a shock to think of Carlotta as Lady Ordeyne) matronly and inefficient, but the joy and delight of every wounded man.

And Septimus? Did you not know that the Dix gun was used at the front? His great new invention, the aero-tank, I regret to say, was looked on coldly by the War Office. Now that Peace has come he is trying, so Brigadier-General Sir Clem Sypher tells me, to adapt it to the intensive cultivation of whitebait.

And I have heard a few stories of others. Here is one told me by a French officer, one Colonel Girault. The scene was a road bridge on the outskirts of the zone of the armies. His car had broken down hopelessly, and with much profane language he swung to the bridge-head. The sentry saluted. He was an elderly Territorial with a ragged pair of canvas trousers and a ragged old blue uniform coat and a battered kepi and an ancient rifle. A scarecrow of a sentry, such as were seen on all the roads of France.

"How far is it to the village?"

"Two kilometres, *mon Colonel*."

There was something familiar in the voice and in the dark, humorous eyes.

"Say, *mon vieux*, what is your name?" asked Colonel Girault.

"Gaston de Nérac, *mon Colonel*."

"*Connais pas*," murmured the Colonel, turning away.

"Exalted rank makes Gigi Girault forget the lessons of humility he learned in the Café Delphine."

Colonel Girault stood with mouth agape. Then he laughed and threw himself into the arms of the dilapidated sentry.

"*Mon Dieu*! It is true. It is Paragot!"

Then afterwards: "And what can I do for you, *mon vieux*?"

"Nothing," said Paragot. "The *bon Dieu* has done everything. He has allowed me to be a soldier of France in my old age."

And Colonel Girault told me that he asked for news of the little Asticot—a painter who ought by now to be famous. Paragot replied:

"He is over there, killing Boches for his old master."

Do you remember Paul Savelli, the Fortunate Youth? He lived to see his dream of a great, awakened England come true. He fell leading his men on a glorious day. His Princess wears on her nurse's uniform the Victoria Cross which he had earned in that last heroic charge, but did not live to wear. And she walks serene and gracious, teaching proud women how to mourn.

What of Quixtus? He sacrificed his leisure to the task of sitting in a dim room of the Foreign Office for ten hours a day in front of masses of German publications, and scheduling with his scientific method and accuracy the German lies. Clementina saw him only on Sundays. She turned her beautiful house on the river into a maternity home for soldiers' wives. Tommy, the graceless, when last home on leave, said that she was capable of murdering the mothers so as to collar all the babies for herself. And Clementina smiled as though acknowledging a compliment. "Once every few years you are quite intelligent, Tommy," she replied.

I have heard, too, that Simon, who jested so with life, and Lola of the maimed face, went out to a Serbian hospital, and together won through the horror of the retreat. They are still out there, sharing in Serbia's victory, and the work of Serbia's reconstruction.

In the early days of the war, in Regent Street, I was vehemently accosted by a little man wearing the uniform of a French captain. He had bright eyes, and a clean shaven chin which for the moment perplexed me, and a swaggering moustache.

"Just over for a few hours to see the wife and little Jean."

"But," said I, "what are you doing in this kit? You went out as a broken-down Territorial."

"*Mon cher ami*," he cried, straddling across the pavement to the obstruction of traffic, and regarding me mirthfully, "it is the greatest farce on the world. Imagine me! I, a broken-down Territorial, as you call me, bearded a lion of a General of Division in his den—and I came out a Captain. Come into the Café Royal and I'll tell you all about it."

His story I cannot set down here, but it is not the least amazing of the joyous adventures of my friend Aristide Pujol.

What Doggie and Jeanne did in the war, my gentle readers know. Their first child was born on the glorious morning of November 11, 1918, amid the pealing of bells and shouts of rejoicing. When Doggie crept into the Sacred Room of Wonderment, he found the babe wrapped up in the Union Jack and the Tricolour. "There's only one name for him," whispered Jeanne with streaming eyes, "Victor!"

To leave fantasy for the brutal fact. You may say these friends of mine are but shadows. It is true. But shadows are not cast by nothingness. These friends must live substantially and corporeally, although in the flesh I have never met them. Some strange and unguessed sun has cast their shadows across my path. I *know* that somewhere or the other they have their actual habitation, and I know that they have done the things I have above recounted. These shadows of things unseen are real. In fable lies essential truth. These shadows that now pass quivering before my eyes have behind them great, pulsating embodiments of men and women, in England and France, who have given up their lives to the great work which is to cleanse the foulness of the Central Empires of Europe, regenerate humanity, and bring Freedom to God's beautiful earth.

THE END

****

BY THE SAME AUTHOR

IDOLS

JAFFERY

VIVIETTE

SEPTIMUS

DERELICTS

THE USURPER

STELLA MARIS

WHERE LOVE IS

THE ROUGH ROAD

THE RED PLANET

THE WHITE DOVE

SIMON THE JESTER

A STUDY IN SHADOWS

A CHRISTMAS MYSTERY

THE WONDERFUL YEAR

THE FORTUNATE YOUTH

THE BELOVED VAGABOND

AT THE GATE OF SAMARIA

THE GLORY OF CLEMENTINA

THE MORALS OF MARCUS ORDEYNE

THE DEMAGOGUE AND LADY PHAYRE

THE JOYOUS ADVENTURES OF ARISTIDE PUJOL

ABOUT THE AUTHOR

WILLIAM JOHN LOCKE

William John Locke (20 March 1863 – 15 May 1930) was a British novelist, dramatist and playwright, best known for his short stories.

He was born in Cunningsbury St George, Christ Church, Demerara, British Guiana on 20 March 1863, the eldest son of John Locke, bank manager of Barbados, and his first wife, Sarah Elizabeth Locke (née Johns). His parents were English. In 1864 his family moved to Trinidad and Tobago. In 1865, a second son was born, Charlie Alfred Locke, who was eventually to become a doctor. Charlie Locke died in 1904 aged 39. His half-sister, Anna Alexandra Hyde (née Locke), by his father's second marriage, died in 1898 in childbirth aged 25.

At the age of three, Locke was sent to England for further education. He remained in England for nine years, before returning to Trinidad to attend prep school with his brother at Queen's Royal College. There, he won an exhibition to enter St John's College, Cambridge. He returned to England in 1881 to attend Cambridge University, where he graduated with honours in Mathematics in 1884, despite his dislike of that "utterly futile and inhuman subject".

After leaving Cambridge, Locke became a schoolmaster. He disliked teaching, but is known to have been a master at the Oxford Military College at Temple Cowley, in 1889 and 1890, and at Clifton College, Bristol in 1890; from 1891 to 1897 he was modern languages master at Trinity College, Glenalmond. In 1893 he published a school edition of Murat, an extract from the Celebrated Crimes (Les crimes célèbres) of Alexandre Dumas père. In 1890 he became seriously ill with tuberculous, which affected him for the rest of his life. From 1897 to 1907 he was secretary of the Royal Institute of British Architects and lived in London. In 1894 he published his first novel, At the Gate of Samaria, but he did not achieve real success for another decade, with The Morals of Marcus Ordeyne (1905) and The Beloved Vagabond (1906). Chambers Biographical Dictionary wrote of his "long series of novels and plays which with their charmingly written sentimental themes had such a success during his life in both Britain and America.... His plays, some of which were dramatised versions of his novels, were all produced with success on the London Stage" (p. 836).

On 19 May 1911, Locke married Aimee Maxwell Close (née Heath), the divorced wife of Percy Hamilton Close, in Chelsea in London. The wedding was attended by Alice Baines and James Douglas.

Five times Locke's books made the list of best-selling novels in the United States for the year. His works have been made into 24 motion pictures the most recent of which was Ladies in Lavender, filmed in 2004 and starring Dame Judi Dench and Maggie Smith. Adapted to the screen by Charles Dance, it was based on Locke's 1916 short story of the same title that had been published in a collection entitled "Faraway Stories." Probably the most famous of Locke's books adapted to the screen was the 1918 Pickford Film Corporation production of Stella Maris starring Mary Pickford. In addition, four of his books were made into Broadway plays, two of which Locke wrote and were produced by Charles Frohman.

Locke died of cancer at 67 rue Desbordes Valmore, Paris, France, on 15 May 1930.

Printed in Great Britain
by Amazon

41394591R00128